TAKING A GAMBLE
OF A KIND

Kalissa Alexander

MENAGE EVERLASTING

Siren Publishing, Inc.
www.SirenPublishing.com

A SIREN PUBLISHING BOOK
IMPRINT: Ménage Everlasting

TAKING A GAMBLE ON THREE OF A KIND
Copyright © 2013 by Kalissa Alexander

ISBN: 978-1-62242-957-8

First Printing: April 2013

Cover design by Harris Channing
All art and logo copyright © 2013 by Siren Publishing, Inc.

ALL RIGHTS RESERVED: This literary work may not be reproduced or transmitted in any form or by any means, including electronic or photographic reproduction, in whole or in part, without express written permission.

All characters and events in this book are fictitious. Any resemblance to actual persons living or dead is strictly coincidental.

Printed in the U.S.A.

PUBLISHER
Siren Publishing, Inc.
www.SirenPublishing.com

TAKING A GAMBLE ON THREE OF A KIND

KALISSA ALEXANDER
Copyright © 2013

Chapter One

Jenny observed the worried frown on her mother's lips as she pressed the *ignore* button on her cell phone. They were eating dinner, but nevertheless, her mother rarely ever ignored a call. As a realtor, the telephone was the lifeline to her business, especially in times like these, when according to her mother, selling a house was the exception and not the rule.

"Everything okay, Mom?" Jenny asked between mouthfuls of her mother's garlic mashed potatoes that she loved.

"Everything's fine, dear. Just someone I can call back later. It's been too long since I had a sit-down dinner with my daughter. I want to spend time with you without work or anything else interrupting us."

"Well, now that the semester is over, you'll be seeing a lot more of me. I know you want me to work with you, but I've got a few leads on jobs for the summer. One is at the Cultural Center in Parsons Grove."

"I know I don't have enough work to keep you busy full-time. I thought you were going to call Elizabeth Andrews's office? I thought she was looking to hire someone. The insurance business seems to be booming."

"I called already. Besides, insurance isn't my thing."

Another call came in on her mother's cell phone. Her mother once again pressed the *ignore* button.

"Maybe you should take that. They must really want to talk to you if they've called twice in such a short period of time."

"Nope. Last year I only saw you for Thanksgiving and Christmas. I know your job as a research assistant has kept you busy and away from home these last few summers, and believe me, I'm glad you've had the opportunity, but I just couldn't take another summer with you being away. I've really missed my daughter. You have no idea how glad I am to have you home finally."

"Well, you did insist that I come home. I mean, not that I didn't want to. But your last message about my living expenses and helping you over the summer did get my attention. So tell me all about you, Mom. Is there a problem with your business? And are you still seeing Jack Rowan?"

Jenny watched her mother's face turn slightly red. She wished her mother felt more comfortable with dating, or maybe she just felt uncomfortable talking about her boyfriend with her daughter. It had been five years since her father had died. When she had discovered her mother was finally seeing someone, she couldn't have been happier. Marlene Clayton was only in her early fifties—way too young to be by herself. Although she was an only child, Jenny prided herself on not being one of those daughters who hated the thought of her mother dating.

"Business could always be better, and Jack and I just enjoy each other's company. It's nothing serious."

"You've always been the number-one realtor around here. I'm sure if business is down, it will pick up and you'll be fine. And I for one am glad that you're still seeing Dr. Rowan. I always liked him growing up. I was sorry when his wife died of cancer."

"It was sad for him and his boys."

"Speaking of his boys, how are they?"

"The twins are through medical school and have come back to help their father. Jack's really happy that they both wanted to take over his medical practice. He says he wants to retire, but I don't think he will. He loves being a doctor way too much."

"If I remember, Adam and Luke were always pretending to be doctors. They tried to examine me once, but Dad put an end to that." She laughed.

"They were both little buggers but harmless. They've grown into nice young men. They'll make some girl very happy."

"You think they'll take the same woman, like most of the men in our town?"

"Yes, I think they might. They don't have to. Their mother and father opted for just each other as your father and I did. But we're not the norm. Most of the families in Brilliance enjoy more polygamous lifestyles."

"Most places are like that now since the government made what was thought of as unconventional marriages legal. However, I liked not having to share my time between more than two parents."

"Well, it's a matter of choice and whatever works for you, dear, whether you take one, two, or more men to be your husband or husbands. There's no pressure here. I just want you to be happy."

"I want the same for you, Mom. How much time are you spending with Jack?" Again, she could see the discomfort on her mother's face. "I know I haven't exactly been around much, so I would imagine you get lonely."

"It does get lonely sometimes. But I'm not about to replace your father, don't you worry. I can't just retire and live a life of leisure…no matter what Jack wants."

"Ah, so you have been seeing a lot of him."

"Well, I guess there's no harm in your knowing that he asked me to marry him. I said no. I can't marry anyone. It just wouldn't be right."

"And you don't call that serious?

"He's much more serious than I am. Let's talk about something else."

"Why? I mean, he's a wonderful man who can make your retirement years fun. You don't have to marry him if you don't want to. I'm sure he'd be fine with a companion. You've got enough money to travel whenever you want. You wouldn't have to depend on him financially. Dad's only been gone five years. I'm sure he understands."

"I don't want to talk about me. Let's talk about you."

"Mom," Jenny said with a slight whine. "Don't do that."

"Do what?"

"Try and change the subject when you don't want to tell me something."

Her mother pushed herself away from the table and stood up. "Well, I guess spending time with him was better than being alone all the time." She took her plate out to the kitchen.

Jenny immediately felt shamed for questioning her mother. She had never made her feel guilty about being away before.

When her mother returned, she sat down and put her head in her hands. "I'm sorry I snapped at you. I always wanted you to be free to do what you wanted without worrying about me. I should have never said that."

"What's wrong, Mom?"

"I need to tell you what I've done. Then you'll understand why I needed you to come home."

"What do you mean, what you've done?" *At least she's not ill.*

"I so didn't want to have to tell you," her mother said, lifting her head up, her watery eyes making contact with Jenny's. "I thought I could fix it, but the more I tried, the worse it got."

"Just tell me. It can't be that bad."

"You can decide once you've heard what I have to say," her mother said, looking down at her lap.

Jenny remained silent and waited for her mother to continue.

"I'm in trouble…financial trouble." Her mother's voice shook. "I've run up all my credit cards, and I've spent all the money your father left us including his insurance money."

"What?" Jenny couldn't have heard her right. They weren't rich by any means, but her father had left them enough money to more than get by on.

"You know that new casino that opened in Carlton?" her mother asked, not expecting an answer. "Well, I started going there after you went to school. I guess I was bored. Not that this has anything to do with you," she added quickly. "I only went once in a while at first, and then at some point I started going more often. I won, but I lost, too, and as time went on, the losses started piling up. I kept thinking I would get back what I lost, but before I knew it, I was taking out money from our savings account and the more I took, thinking I would win, the more I lost. I have nothing left, Jenny. I should say, we having nothing left. I'm so sorry."

Jenny put down her fork and just stared at her mother who had tears running unheeded down her cheeks. She couldn't believe what she was hearing. This was crazy. She had never known her mother to ever set foot inside a casino, let alone be a regular customer.

"When you say there's nothing left, do you mean you spent *all* the money gambling?"

"That's what I said. I know it's hard to believe. There was over two hundred thousand dollars in that account. I can't believe it either. I was like another person. Those damn slot machines were all I could think about. I've ruined everything. I even took out a second mortgage. I'm going to lose this house, and I don't even have the money to help you with your housing for next year.

Jenny was speechless. Nothing could have prepared her for this. It was insane.

"Say something, anything," her mother choked out.

"I don't know what to say."

"I kept telling myself that since your tuition as a PhD student was paid by the school, you would be fine. Then, I remembered that you weren't eligible for a stipend in your fifth year and you'd need twice to three times as much from me as you have in the past. I don't have it to give," her mother all but cried. "You must hate me."

"I just don't understand how you could have spent all the money."

"I'm so sorry."

"Well, sorry isn't going to pay the bills is it?" Jenny shouted louder than she had intended. "I need to get out of here. Otherwise I'm going to start screaming, and that won't solve anything."

"I wish I'd never seen a slot machine. You don't know how many times I've gone over what I did in my head. It seems surreal, like I'm someone else, not me. If I could give my life to get it all back, I would."

"Don't go there," Jenny said sharply. "That would be the ultimate selfishness."

Jenny couldn't bear to look at her mother another second. She grabbed her mother's car keys before she left the house. She needed a drink, not that she was drinker, but after the bombshell her mother had just dropped on her, she might become one. She drove in circles for at least fifteen minutes until she remembered a bar she and her girlfriends frequented when they were in high school. The bartender at the time never asked for ID. Not that it was a problem now. But even at twenty-six, she still got carded.

When she pulled up to the Medusa, she didn't think she was going to find a spot to park, but someone was leaving, and she pulled in as they pulled out. She never went into a bar alone, but tonight would be the exception. She opened the door and walked into the dimly lit interior filled with smoke and a country song blasting so loud, she wondered how anyone could stand it. Most places didn't allow smoking anymore, but this place had never been one to follow the rules.

She found an empty barstool and sat down. The bartender came over to her, giving her a lecherous look that made her skin crawl. The guy was old enough to be father and had creepy eyes. "What'll it be, sweetie?"

"I'll have a beer, whatever kind you have, I don't care."

"Well, we have a few, but I'll pick out a good one for you." He winked.

When he placed a bottle in front of her without a glass, she just smiled. She wasn't about to ask him for anything else. She wanted him gone. She wasn't even wearing any makeup, and he was staring at her like she his favorite toy. Thankfully, someone from the other end of the bar yelled for him.

"Gotta go, sweet thing, but you let me know if you want anything else," he leered, his meaning more than clear.

She turned and took a sip of her beer. She heard him laugh as he walked away.

Looking around, she focused on the dance floor in the corner that was filled to capacity. Everyone appeared to be in good spirits. Just this morning, she was happy, too. Looking away, she tried to calm herself. All she wanted to do was forget the last hour of her life. Before dinner she was pretty much carefree, spending an obligatory summer at home knowing she would be back to school for her final year. Now she felt like not only had the rug had been swept out from under her, but the mother she had always depended on was far from dependable. How could someone who had always been so frugal have gone through all that money so quickly? It was beyond her comprehension.

Pushing her dark auburn hair behind her ears and out of her face, she closed her eyes. Would they really lose the house? They must be close to it or her mother would have never told her what she had done. Like it or not, she was going to have to be the adult here and figure something out, that is if it wasn't already too late.

She opened her eyes and glanced up at the television behind the bar. Some news show came across the screen, but the volume had been muted. Pictures depicting a house fire caught her attention. She was so fixated on the burning building she didn't realize someone was calling her name until she felt a nudge against her arm.

"Jenny Clayton, is that you?"

At first she couldn't place the handsome man staring down at her and then it hit her. Luke Rowan continued to stare at her with a big grin and deep-set blue eyes that were sparkling with what appeared to be humor. He was older and, if possible, even more handsome than he was in high school. He was one of the last people she wanted to run into. His father wanted to marry her mother. Well, at least he thought he did.

"Luke," she said, pretending to be happy to see him. "How nice to see you."

"So you do remember me?"

"Of course I do. Is your brother here, too?"

"Adam's around. The last time I saw him he was dancing with April Mathews. You remember her, don't you?"

How could she forget April? The cheerleader, Homecoming Queen, and all-around girl next door with a superior attitude that had been the envy of every girl in high school. She thought she'd be married with kids by now and not out dancing with the Rowan brothers.

"Just because I've been away at school doesn't mean I don't remember people. My mother tells me you're working with your father now."

"Yup. Adam and are both helping Dad with his practice. He needs to retire and live it up a little. Keep hoping your mother will agree to marry him. She's pretty stubborn. Not that much unlike you if I remember that dance you took a fit over."

Luke and Adam had been seniors when she was a freshman and in a totally different social group, but they had always been cordial to her whenever they happened to run into each other. She had been without a date for the Spring Fling, and her mother had asked the Rowan brothers to be her date. She had been mortified, but pleased that they had said they would. However, her father had been livid. She had heard her mother and father fighting, which was something they never did. She had come out of her room and stood at the top of the stairs where their voices had carried up to her.

"You know as well as I do that those boys are seniors and shouldn't be within ten feet of a freshman, especially my daughter. She's no match for them. I can't believe you asked them to take her the dance."

"They're good boys, and Jack said he thought it was a fine idea."

"I'm sure he did. He thinks those boys can do no wrong. I'm not going to have them break my daughter's heart or worse. She's far too good for them, and I'm not giving them a free card to use her. Boys their age like nothing better than to take advantage of an innocent girl like Jenny. Don't think I haven't seen the way they look at her."

"Come on, Carl. You're not serious. They would never hurt Jenny."

"They're Rowans and that's all I'm going to say."

Immediately her mother's voice had lowered, and Jenny couldn't hear her response. The next day her mother had called Jack and told him it was Jenny that had said no to the dance. What excuse she had used, she didn't know. The unwanted memory brought with it the warmth of embarrassment that crept upward from her neck, making her wish the memory could have stayed buried along with the crush she had secretly harbored for the twins.

She knew Luke was waiting for a response. Not taking the bait, she said, "You guys come here often?"

"It's a good place to blow off a little steam, and the drinks are cheap," he said with a laugh, leaning in closer to her. The woman sitting next to her smiled at them before she inched off the stool and walked toward a neon sign that flashed "Women."

"You coming back?" Luke shouted to the woman's retreating back.

Turning, she smiled. "Nope. Sit down and enjoy yourself, handsome."

Luke gave her a wink and a wave before he turned back to Jenny and sat down.

"You don't mind if I sit here next to you, do you, Jenny?"

Would it matter if I did? "Please yourself."

"Most times I do. Thanks. We've got some catching up to do," he said, his eyes slowly appraising her from head to toe. "You've grown up nicely since we used to play doctor." Jenny couldn't believe that Luke had just made reference to something she had assumed he had forgotten about long ago. She couldn't stop herself from wondering what it would be like to play doctor with him now, since he was one. Feeling the heat of embarrassment crawl up her neck, she turned her interest back to her beer and away from the handsome man that was making her stomach do unwanted flip-flops.

Chapter Two

Luke held up his empty beer bottle. The bartender nodded in acknowledgement and returned with a new bottle and took the old one. "Glad to see you've got some company, little lady," he said, giving Jenny a knowing smile.

"Old friends," Luke said. He was smiling, but it didn't quite reach his eyes. The bartender turned and walked away. "Watch out for that guy. He loves the ladies, especially the ones that are beautiful and young. He's a chronic flirt."

"And you aren't? That crack about playing doctor with me wasn't meant to be flirtatious?" Jenny asked sarcastically.

"I didn't realize I was flirting. But if you want me to, I can oblige."

"Don't talk stupid, Luke," Jenny said, wishing he'd go away and leave her alone. "I'm not in the mood for it."

"Damn. What are you in the mood for?"

"Not for your kind of entertainment, that's for sure." Normally she would have never been so rude. But nothing about today had been normal, and she was still reeling from her mother's confession. She wasn't about to sit here and let Luke Rowan have his fun at her expense, regardless of how many times she had dreamed of him and his brother giving her more than the time of day when she was still a wide-eyed, innocent kid.

"Damn, the kitten's got claws. But I'm not averse to a little pain if the end result gets me what I want," he said silkily. "But just to put your mind at ease, I'm not interested in getting you into bed if that's what you think. One Clayton woman in the family is enough. No disrespect toward your mother, but not sure sleeping with her daughter would help my father's cause."

"I'm certainly going to sleep better tonight knowing I'm off your radar."

"You're not disappointed, are you?"

The humorous glint in his eyes made her want to slap his face. When did he get so damn arrogant? Maybe he always had been and she just hadn't noticed.

Luke was just about to continue the conversation she was hoping to end, when a large hand planted itself on his shoulder. He looked up. "Hey, Adam. Look who I ran into," Luke said, turning back toward Jenny.

"Jenny Clayton," Adam said with a smile. "Your mother told me you were coming home from school. She's really missed you. You're all she talks about."

"Really?"

"Whenever I see her, she's always singing your praises. I understand you've done very well in school. She was worried you might not want to come home for the summer. I'm glad you did. She missed you a lot."

"Well, I was busy with school. I had things I had to do." She knew he wasn't trying to make her feel guilty, or at least she didn't think he was. She knew now that she should have never stayed away from home so long at a stretch, but she had her reasons. However, if she hadn't, maybe her mother would have confided in her sooner and things wouldn't have gotten so out of control. But there was little she could do about that now.

Jenny felt another set of eyes on her. For the first time she realized Adam, who resembled Luke but was not identical, had his arm draped around who else but April Mathews. She groaned inwardly. *My night is now complete.* "Hello, Jenny," April said, not smiling. "Fancy running into you in a place like this. I thought you'd be the type to go to more sophisticated places that served those fancy drinks."

Speaking of claws, April certainly hadn't lost hers since she had seen her last, nor had she lost her looks. She was dressed in a tight shirt and short skirt that did nothing to hide her curves. Even her long hair, that was now bleached blonde, was tied back in a ponytail like she had worn in high school. The girl was obviously stuck in the past.

"Hello, April. Nice to see you, too," Jenny said, giving her the same courtesy of not smiling.

Ignoring the two women, Adam said to Luke, "April and I want to go over to The Cedars. They've got a real band, and we thought it would be fun to do some line dancing."

"Sounds good," Luke replied. "But I'm not going unless Jenny comes, too. You remember how to line dance, Jenny?"

Practically everyone in Brilliance knew how to line dance. It was almost a requirement along with knowing how to ride a horse.

"I don't like dancing," she lied.

"Now I know that's a lie," Luke countered, staring her right in the eye. "Your mother told us you won a dancing contest in eighth grade."

Obviously, Adam had been telling the truth about her mother's inability to stop talking about her.

"Good old Mom. Is there nothing she hasn't told you two about me?" *She's certainly kept a lot of things from me, including how close she's gotten with all the Rowan men.*

"So you do like to dance. You just don't want to dance with me, is that it?" Luke's stare was unnerving.

"Leave her alone, Luke. She obviously doesn't want to come with us," April whined, grabbing Luke's arm. "Let's go."

"I said," Luke said pointedly, his eyes never leaving Jenny's, "that I wasn't going unless Jenny comes, too."

She didn't want to go, but she didn't want to sit here at the bar with the bartender waiting to pounce on her either. She also wasn't ready to go home and face her mother. She still wasn't sure what she was going to say to her, not that there were a lot of options. Making her feel worse than she already did wasn't something she would take any pleasure in doing. She loved her mother, but right now she didn't like her much.

"Give me directions. I'll follow you there."

"Adam and I came here together with April. I'll ride with you. That way I can make sure you don't get lost."

"Smart man," Adam said. "We'll see you there."

Adam and April walked away from them and toward the door. Luke put some bills down on the counter.

"I can pay for my own drink."

"I'm sure you can. But I'm paying for it. No argument."

Arrogant and bossy. He obviously was used to getting his own way. She didn't want to cause a scene, and it was only one beer. She picked up her purse that was hanging on the hook under the bar before she stood up. Luke draped his arm across her shoulders. He must have felt her stiffen.

She felt his breath on her ear. "Just directing you toward the door and through the crowd," he said, bringing her body closer to his.

As soon as they were out the door, Jenny moved away from him. "My car's over here," she said, walking in front of him.

"Yes, ma'am," he said mocking her.

She pulled out the keys from her purse and pushed the button to unlock the doors. Luke moved in front of her and opened the passenger-side door and grabbed the keys from her hand. He walked quickly to the driver's side.

"You're not driving," Jenny said, wondering who he thought he was.

"I'm driving," he said, his hand on the door handle. "I know where we're going and it will be easier this way. You can relax and enjoy the ride. Besides," he said snidely, "this way you won't have to worry about what I'm doing with my hands."

"I thought you said you weren't interested in getting me in bed, not that you'd have any luck in that department."

"I did say that, didn't I?" he asked, opening the door. "However, I've been known to change my mind. Best that I drive."

"You really are something, Luke Rowan. Give me the keys and stop bossing me around."

He continued to look at her with an innocent smile on his face. "I'm doing this for your own good." He slid into the driver's seat and shut the door behind him.

And he called her stubborn. Sighing, she slid into the passenger seat without looking at him. She slipped on the seat belt and tried to stay calm. Luke was a forceful man who liked to take charge. She'd be lying if she said he didn't turn her on, however, he was a Rowan and that complicated everything. All she wanted to do was relax and forget her troubles for a little while and although she was hard-pressed to admit it, maybe Luke was what she needed tonight. She could feel the tension leaving her body.

* * * *

Adam and April had already found them a table when she and Luke entered The Cedars. Most everyone was dressed in costume. Lots of leather, fringe, and cowboy boots. She looked down at her jeans and high heels. She wasn't even sure she could dance in these shoes.

"You look great. Those shoes really show off those long, lovely legs of yours," Luke whispered in her ear before pulling out a chair for her.

Once again she thought about a time when she would have loved for either one or both of the brothers to have said something like that to her. However, times had changed, and she wasn't that girl any longer. She liked being free to choose and do as she liked where men were concerned. She had never been in love and was glad now more than ever. If loving someone like her mother had her father was the catalyst for such an abrupt change in personality when they were taken away, she wasn't sure she ever wanted to give another person the power to destroy her like that.

"Things are in full swing here," Adam said, laughing at his play on words.

"Adam, sometimes you're so corny," April said, looking up at him adoringly. "And, you," she said, turning to Luke, "were such a gentleman to make sure Jenny found the place."

"Hey, that's us. Corny gentlemen," Luke said, giving Adam a conspiratorial wink.

Jenny turned her head toward the dancers and away from April, who was practically sitting in Adam's lap. She hadn't been out dancing in a long time. She found herself enjoying the way the men and women moved with such grace and precision.

"When this dance is over, I'm dragging you out on the dance floor if I have to," Luke said as the waitress approached their table. He ordered beers for all them. What if she hadn't wanted a beer? Luke was way too sure of himself for her. The song ended and many of the dancers dispersed. However, a good many stayed put, waiting for the next song.

Good to his word, Luke grabbed her hand. She didn't feel like being dragged, so she followed him onto the dance floor. However, he turned and looked down at her feet.

"Kick them off. Barefoot is better."

She hated to admit that he was probably right. Her heels were way too high for dancing. She slid them off and kicked them toward their table. April and Adam walked right in front her.

"Whoa, there," Adam said, dodging a shoe. "Those things are dangerous."

April just shook her head and pulled Adam out onto the dance floor and away from Jenny and Luke. For some reason she felt incredibly nervous, and that made her mind go blank. She froze. Thankfully something clicked in her brain just as the music started and she found her feet moving in sync with Luke's—right, left behind right, right again, and then the left meets the right. She repeated the steps, adding to them as the dance progressed.

Luke was an excellent dance partner. They had only danced a few dances before she begged him to let her rest. "I think I'm out of shape," she said breathlessly.

"It's like riding a bike. Once you learn how, you never forget."

Jenny nodded, grateful he was leading her off the dance floor and back to their table. She picked up her shoes before she sat down. She slipped them back on.

"You need a pair of boots."

"I have a couple pairs. I just haven't worn them in a long time."

She lifted her bottle of beer to her lips and practically emptied it. She hadn't realized how thirsty she was. The waitress was passing by and Luke ordered another round for the table.

"So," he said, bringing his attention back to her, "when do you have to go back to school?"

His question should have been an easy one, but in light of the evening's revelations, it almost brought tears to her eyes. She wasn't going back to school. The thought hit her like a ton of bricks. She stared at the beer bottle before she lifted it to her lips.

"It's not a trick question, Jenny."

"I think I'm going to sit this next year out. Take a break."

"Does your mother know?" He asked with what seemed like real concern.

"Yes. She does and she agrees with me."

"Really?"

"Yes, really. We have some things we need to work out together. Missing a year of school isn't the end of the world. Students going for their doctorate in art history don't always finish in four or five years. Some go as long as eight."

"Is that what you want? Funny that your mother never mentioned you weren't going back at dinner the other night."

"She has dinner with you guys a lot, does she?"

"Doesn't she tell you anything about us?

"No, not really."

"That's a little strange," he said, looking at her as if she were somehow to blame. "Well, she comes over a couple times a week. Dad takes her out for dinner, too. They enjoy being together. It makes no sense to me why she won't marry him unless there's an obstacle she hasn't told him about."

"She still misses my dad. I'm not sure she'll ever get remarried."

"My dad misses my mother, too, but being alone for the rest of your life when there's someone who you care for that wants to be with you, that's crazy. She needs to move on."

"That's one of the reasons why I'm not going back to school."

"What do you mean?"

"The moving on part. She does need to move on, and I'm going to help her do it."

Luke was silent for a moment. "Am I missing something here? I get the feeling you're holding something back."

Jenny shook her head. She wasn't about to tell him that her life was in ruins and moving on could mean moving away from the home she had always loved. "No. Just that she needs me now and I'm going to be here for her."

Again, Luke just stared at her. "Do you not like my dad?"

"Your dad's a great guy. Of course I like him. I always have."

"Sounds like you might be trying to break them up or something."

"You're way overanalyzing this conversation," she said guardedly. "Whatever our parents do, it's their decision. I'm not my mother's keeper."

"Good. I'd hate to see two nice people like them break up because of something or someone acting stupid."

Silently they watched the dancers. Several dances later, Adam and April came back to the table. April downed the one beer and picked up the other bottle Luke had ordered for her.

"I do love to dance," April said with a giggle. "Now it's your turn, Luke." April jumped up from the chair and held her hand toward Luke. "I want to dance with you now."

"Duty calls," Luke called over his shoulder as he let April lead him out onto the dance floor.

Adam sat next to her and stretched his legs. "I like to dance, but taking a break is nice, too, but if you want to dance…"

"No. I'm fine just watching."

"I like your hair long. You always used to wear it in a bob or something like that."

"Thanks. My dad liked it short. But I like it longer now."

"Everything okay with you and Luke?"

"Sure. Why wouldn't it be?"

"I don't know. I looked over your way a few times, and it looked like you two were involved in a pretty heavy conversation."

"I told him I wasn't going back to school and he read a lot more into it than was necessary. That's all."

"You're not going back to school? Why?"

"If you don't mind, Adam. I'm talked out about school. Luke can fill you in later. It's no big deal."

"It doesn't sound like it's no big deal, but if you don't want to talk about it, we'll talk about something else."

Jenny smiled. Adam was obviously still the quieter, less aggressive twin. He was equally as handsome, but he didn't have Luke's edginess. "So tell me about your medical practice with your Dad. What made you two decide to come back to Brilliance? I thought you both might practice at some city hospital."

"We thought about it. We could have, we had offers, but we both agreed that we wanted to come home to Brilliance. We love it here and it's a growing place, even with the economy being so bad. There's a future here, and besides that, it's home."

"I did see a few new developments here and there, but according to my mom, the real estate business has been in a downward spiral."

"That's true in most places, but I got the impression from my dad that your mother's been one of the lucky ones. I mean, she's pretty busy, keeps a lot of late nights with clients. Those developments you saw, she's the one that's been selling them."

"She doesn't like to brag," Jenny said quickly. Something wasn't right. If her mother's business was doing so well, why couldn't she pay her bills? *Unless, she is still gambling.*

Chapter Three

The thought that her mother could still be going to the casino stayed with her for the rest of the evening. She danced with both the brothers and tolerated April's dirty looks when she wasn't insulting her. It was pretty obvious that she had set her sights on both brothers and Jenny wasn't a welcome addition to the evening.

"So I guess you're going to be around all summer. Bet you can't wait to get back to school," April said from across the table. Adam and Luke had gone to the men's room leaving the two women alone.

Jenny groaned inside. She didn't want to tell April anything, but she couldn't ignore her question without being blatantly rude, and that wasn't in her nature. "I'm going to take a break from school."

"No," April said, her eyes widening in surprise. "Why would you want to do that?"

"Just some things I need to take care of here at home, and I need a break. Don't worry, I'll be busy working so I won't be crashing any of your dates with the twins."

"I'm not worried." April shrugged. "You got nothing those boys want. Luke's just a flirt. But when the lights are out and the covers are down, he knows where he belongs."

"I'm sure he does," Jenny said, wishing Luke and Adam would hurry back and save her from further conversation with their girlfriend.

"Besides, from what I hear, you're practically family. When their daddy marries your mother, they'll be your stepbrothers. I'll be your stepsister-in-law. Won't that be a hoot," she said with a giggle that turned into laughter.

"Glad to see you two girls are getting along," Adam said, sliding back into his seat next to April. Luke sat back down next to Jenny.

"What's so funny?" Luke asked.

"Nothing we want to share with you boys," April said quickly. "Just girl talk."

"Is that right," Luke said, looking pointedly at Jenny.

"Girls do talk," she said, playing along with April, who obviously wasn't as sure of the twins as she would like Jenny to believe. Otherwise, she would have shared her observation about their upcoming family ties as she saw them.

The rest of the evening Jenny spent with her shoes off and her feet dancing. The more she danced, the more she realized how much she had missed it. She had regained her second wind, and although she had thought the evening was going to be a bust, she was having fun. It was exactly what she needed to take her mind off her mother.

When the last song was over, Luke insisted on driving her home. She was too tired to argue or drive. Adam and April followed in Adam's Lexus. *Obviously someone is doing well financially.*

She expected Luke to continue taunting her, but instead he was quiet and kept his eyes on the road. When she did look over at him, he looked her way briefly and smiled. He turned on her radio and they listened to music until he pulled up in front of her house. The porch light was on.

Luke jumped out of the car and opened her door for her. For some reason she was having trouble with her seat belt. She felt him lean across her chest, brushing up against her breasts. She could feel her nipples harden. For a moment, she wanted to reach out and stop him from pulling away from her, but that, she knew, would not be in her best interest. Instead, she took his hand that he offered her to help her out of the car. His hand then cupped her elbow. She found herself leaning into him. She really was exhausted.

"I think I may have worn you out, Jenny Clayton," Luke said softly.

"I'm going to go to sleep as soon as my head hits the pillow," she smiled.

"Now that you're home, I'm sure we'll be seeing a lot more of you. Don't beg off the family dinners. It will hurt your mother."

Jenny's head snapped up. Family dinners? That was news to her. "Right. Thanks for the advice," she said sarcastically, turning to open the door with her key.

"I mean it, Jenny. I expect you to encourage their relationship and not to be a stumbling block."

He was so close she felt slightly off-balance. Her anger helped her to right herself.

"If our parents are meant to be together, there's nothing you or I or anyone else will be able to do to prevent it. So stop giving me orders. I don't like being told what to do."

"I'm not so sure about that," he said silkily, his hand slightly caressing her cheek.

Jenny felt paralyzed. She watched him lower his head. Did he actually have the audacity to kiss her?

His lips hovered above hers. "I'm just a good son who wants his father to be happy. I'm hoping you're a good daughter who wants the same for her mother. I'm very protective of my father. His happiness means everything to me."

"And you think my mother's doesn't mean everything to me?" Whatever magic he had been weaving around her was shattered. All she wanted to do was to smack that arrogant look off his face.

"I think you're an only child who has been spoiled by both your mother and your father. I'm not sure you've ever put anyone else's happiness above your own."

She felt the blood drain from her face. "That's a horrible thing to say. You don't know me."

"I know that you practically ignored your mother these past couple of years, and now that she and my father are close to tying the knot, you're not only home from school but you're staying home. What are you afraid of, Jenny?"

"Certainly not you." She turned from him quickly, feeling tears forming behind her lids. She hated that when she got really angry she had a tendency to cry. It was embarrassing. She saw Adam's car pull in front of her house as she turned the door handle and scooted inside, shutting the door behind her before he could say another word. She leaned against it until she heard Adam's car speed away. Luke had no idea who her mother really was. For that matter, neither did she. But she knew one thing, if her mother was still gambling, she was going to stop. And even if she wasn't, and she highly doubted that, her mother was going to see a professional whether she wanted to or not.

* * * *

When Jenny opened her eyes the next morning, she looked over at the clock on her nightstand. It was eleven thirty. She groaned. She felt like she had been hit by a truck. Swinging her legs off the side of the bed, she massaged her calf muscles. She had really overdone it.

She limped to the shower and turned it on as hot as she could take it. She used the shower massager to loosen her tight muscles. It felt good. When she emerged from the bathroom, she pulled on a pair of jeans and a tank top and padded barefoot down the stairs to the kitchen. Her mother was sitting at the kitchen table with a cup of coffee. As soon as she saw Jenny, she got up and poured her one.

"Where were you last night if you don't mind my asking?"

"I was out dancing with Luke and Adam Rowan."

"You were," she said in surprise. "How did that happen?"

"I went to a bar for a drink, and they were there with April Mathews. They asked me to go dancing with them, so I did."

"Well, that was nice. I wish you had called me. I was worried about you."

"I should have called." Regardless of what her mother had told her, making her worry needlessly wasn't something she was proud of doing.

"All's well then," her mother said, sitting down across from her.

"Really? You think so?"

"Well, you know what I mean. You're safe. You couldn't have been out with nicer boys."

"They're not boys anymore, they're thirty-year-old men, and from the way April was talking, if she has her way, they'll be married men before long."

"That's news to me. I know they go out here and there, but I didn't know they were exclusive with April. I've never seen her at the house."

"And from what Adam tells me, you spend quite a bit of time over there in between running your busy real estate business and frequenting the casino."

"He told you no such thing!" her mother exclaimed in horror. "He knows nothing about the casino."

"No. You're right about that. He knows nothing about the casino. But he did tell me how busy you are. How is it possible that you can't pay my living expenses and we're losing the house unless you're still gambling?" Jenny couldn't help that her voice had risen or that she wanted desperately to shake some sense into her mother.

"I—" her mother began before she burst into tears and brought her hands up to cover her face.

"I'm sorry I'm yelling at you, Mom." Jenny lowered her voice. "It's just I can't believe you're still going there after everything you told me. Why would you do such a thing?"

"I keep thinking"—her mother lowered her hands, wiping her tears on a tissue she removed from the pocket of her slacks—"that I'll get it back. That I can make everything right again."

"You're addicted to it."

"I don't know. I just don't know."

"You're never going back there again, Mom. I swear if you do, I'm going right to Jack Rowan and tell him the truth. And you're going to get professional help. We still have insurance, right?"

"Yes. We do. It's from your father's policy that carried over after he died. I've made sure the premiums were paid."

"Thank God for that." Jenny sighed. "I'll call the insurance company and get a list of doctors that specialize in this kind of thing, and then I'll make you an appointment."

"You don't have to do that. I can do it."

"I'd rather do it myself. I want you to get better, Mom. You have to get better."

"You're right. I've made such a mess of things," she said, the tears flowing once again.

Jenny sat staring at her mother. She wanted to put her arms around her and tell her everything would be okay the way her mother had done when she was a child. But instinctively, she knew she had to be strong, and the one thing she couldn't do was enable her mother to continue this insane behavior that had landed them both into such a financial mess.

"Mom, I need you to promise me you're not going back there."

"I promise. I don't want to go back. I really won't."

"That's a beginning. I want to look over all the bills, checking account statements, and any other accounts you might still have. I need a clear picture of what we're facing. It's the only way to see if there's a way out of this."

Between a couple pots of coffee and sandwiches, the rest of the morning and early afternoon was spent poring over her mother's accounts. Most everything was online, including her checking account. Jenny could see the deductions that were taken out at the casino. They were staggering in the amount and the frequency. She wanted to cry, but that wouldn't change anything. In the end, she knew what had to be done.

If they were to save the house, she had to speak with a few of their creditors to see if she could hopefully lower their interest rates. She also needed to get a real job. Not some summer internship or part-time hourly job, but a full-time job that paid decent money. They still had a small retirement check from her father that went directly into the account that had once held their savings. She could see from her mother's records that her commissions had been rather good of late. However, they weren't always consistent. But even if her mother's commissions remained on the high side, there was no way she could even think about going back to school. The money wasn't there, and in good conscience, she couldn't leave her mother now.

No matter how much she enjoyed living on her own and pursuing her degree, she had no choice but to give up her lease along with the life she had made for herself that was far removed from her life in Brilliance. She was respected by her professors and her peers. Her friends at school were going to be shocked when she told them the news and she would have tell them soon since four of them were living in her apartment over the summer.

Jenny put her pen down and looked across the table at her mother. "It's going to take us a few years to get this under control. But I think we can do it as long as I'm working. We're never going to get back our savings. That's gone. But we can survive as long as you never step foot into another casino or gamble in any way. Do you understand?"

"I do understand, and I'm grateful to you, Jenny. I never wanted you to know how far I'd fallen. I never wanted to burden you with this. The fact that you can't go back to school is killing me."

"Nothing can be done about that now. But we're going to get through this."

"This is the first time I feel like maybe I can beat this thing. But you're right. I need help."

"I'll call tomorrow. We'll find someone you can talk to."

"Could you make it someone who doesn't live in Brilliance?"

"Of course. No one need ever know about this, Mom."

"You won't tell Jack, then?"

"No, I'm not going to tell him anything as long as you're moving in the right direction. Do you love him?" The question just popped out without forethought.

"I've always loved him."

"What do you mean, you've always loved him?"

"I'm sorry. I didn't mean to say that. I'm just not myself."

"You sounded like you knew exactly what you were saying. I want the truth, something we need more of around here."

Her mother sighed. "Okay. You already know that we all grew up here in Brilliance, your father, Jack, and me Your father was a few years older. Jack and I dated before he went away to medical school. When he came back I thought we'd get back together, although he hadn't asked me to wait. When he did come back, he brought Abigail with him, and that was the end of the romance I thought he and I had. Your father and I started dating soon after, and we got married."

"You didn't love Dad? All these years I thought you had the most wonderful marriage. I don't know how much more I can take."

"I loved your father. Not the way I did Jack. But in time I came to love the man he was, and he loved me so much. I never regretted marrying him, and he never knew that I still had feelings for Jack. I want you to believe me. It's the truth."

"I don't know what the truth is anymore." Jenny pushed herself away from the table and ran up to her room, slamming the door like she was eight years old. She couldn't help it. She thought she had found a way to solve one problem, and then her mother told her she had always been in love with Jack Rowan and her father had been her second choice. This was more than any daughter should have to endure.

She knew it was wrong to assume she knew things she didn't, but looking back, she had always sensed that her father had an issue with the Rowans. How could he not have known? How it must have hurt him to know that his wife was in love with another man. And yet he stayed. He was such a good man. He would never turn his back on his family, especially his only child.

Her mother opened her bedroom door without knocking. "Please, don't shut me out. I know I'm a terrible mother, but I love you and I loved your father. I should have never told you about Jack. He doesn't even know how I felt. These past few years with him have been wonderful, but I would give them all back if I could have one more day with your father."

"When did you start seeing Jack?"

"It's been three years now. I think it was right after Thanksgiving."

Jenny brushed past her mother and ran down the stairs and back to the kitchen where she left her notes concerning her mother's accounts.

She turned to see her mother had followed her.

"I want you to stop seeing Jack Rowan."

"Why would you want me to do that? I just told you how I feel about him. None of this has anything to do with him."

"It just occurred to me that you started seeing him right around the time you started going to the casino a lot. There's a direct correlation between him and the escalation of your gambling problem."

"No. That can't be."

"Do the math. It's true. He's no good for you. He never was. I don't know the psychological reason for your irrational need to have him in your life, but there is one. You can't deny the facts. He's done nothing but hurt this family."

Her mother sat down at the table. "It just doesn't seem possible. He's been nothing but good to me. You have to be wrong."

"I'm not. If you want, go back over your statements, you'll see I'm right." Jenny shook her head. "You have to stop seeing him. If you don't, you're not going to get better, and if you don't get better, you're going to have to declare bankruptcy. And if that happens, everyone in Brilliance is going to know about your addictions, including Jack Rowan. Think he'll still want you then?"

"He won't want me. Who would?"

"Mom," Jenny said softly. "I shouldn't have said that. That was cruel. I'm not myself either."

"I deserved it. The truth hurts, but for once I'm going to do the right thing. You needn't worry. I'll break it off with him."

"I know it won't be easy. You have to be strong."

"I forgot to tell you we're invited over there for dinner tomorrow. I guess I should tell him after dinner."

"It might be better if you told him when you two were totally alone. I'm not sure a family dinner is the time or place."

"I know what I've done to you. Taken away from you. I'll never forgive myself. You deserve better."

"Give yourself a couple weeks to tell him. He might think it's strange if you break up with him a few days after I come home. He'll probably still think it's strange, but this way you'll have some time to prepare. I don't you want you to be unhappy, Mom. But this thing with Jack isn't healthy."

"I won't let him think this had anything to do with you. I'm not going to let him blame you for something that's entirely my fault."

Jenny nodded. "Okay, we'll go to dinner tomorrow and we'll smile and act like everything is status quo."

Her mother turned and closed the door behind her. Jenny sat on her bed and wondered how she had become the adult in their relationship. She knew this was going to be difficult for her mother, but Jack had been the catalyst for her mother's illness, she was convinced of it. It was too much of a coincidence. He had also been a thorn in her father's side. There was no way he should be allowed back in her mother's life.

She remembered Luke's parting words to her about not coming between their parents. In his mind, he would think she was responsible for their breakup, but that was something she'd have to deal with. In a way she was breaking them up, but she had no choice.

Tomorrow's dinner would be difficult, but she'd get through it for her mother's sake. She wasn't looking forward to seeing Luke again. Their last encounter on the porch had been anything but pleasant. And it would only get worse once Jack and her mother were no longer seeing each other. She was sure that neither of the brothers would sit idly by and not try to fix it. There was nothing more important to her now than helping her mother get her life back on track, and unfortunately Jack Rowan could never be a part of that life.

Chapter Four

Jenny picked out a blue short-sleeved dress that fell to just above her knees. The skirt was flowing and the neckline squared to show off her bone structure. She opted for a heart-shaped necklace and matching earrings that her father had given her when they went to their first father-daughter dance. If only he were still alive. None of this would have happened.

However, if she were totally honest, her father had never been much for her leaving home to go to school. He had always assumed she would attend the local college. When he died, her mother had told her she could go anywhere she wanted. Something inside of her said she should stay close to home, but another side of her wanted a chance to spread her wings away from the confines of a small town where everyone knew everyone.

Her father had been strict with her, but he had also been watchful with her mother. Maybe he knew she had an addictive personality and had deliberately kept her in check. Fact was, he had kept them both on a pretty tight leash, but that was just his way. He was a good man who had loved his wife and daughter without question. He deserved better than to be a consolation prize. She felt her emotions getting away from her and willed them to stop.

"Jenny, are you almost ready?" Her mother's voice carried through her bedroom door.

"I'll be right down," she shouted.

Slipping into her shoes, she gave herself a once-over in the full-length mirror on the back of her closet door. She had opted to wear her hair down with one side swept up in a comb. Her eye makeup had been applied carefully to make her large, almond-shaped green eyes look even larger and her long lashes thicker. Pleased with her appearance, she opened the door and went downstairs. This, she told herself, as she stepped into the foyer, might be the last time she would have a civil conversation with any of the Rowan men, so she might as well try and look nice.

"You look beautiful, Jenny," her mother said, walking toward her down the hall from the kitchen. "That necklace you're wearing…your father gave it to you."

"Yes, he did. It makes me feel a little closer to him."

"He loved you very much."

The last thing she wanted to do was start crying. She said, "You look nice, too." Her mother did look lovely. She was quite striking when she dressed up and applied makeup. Their hair was the same color, except now that her mother dyed hers, it was a few shades lighter. She wore it in a short style that she said was easy to keep up. Jenny liked it. She could see why Dr. Rowan would be taken with her mother. However, in their youth, he had opted for another woman. Jenny still found her mother's last revelation hard to accept. She hated that her father had been her mother's second choice. Had he somehow known? Was that why he was so strict and unyielding at times?

"Jenny," her mother said, coming to stand beside her. "Are you okay? I mean I know this is an imposition for you. Putting on an act for my sake. I appreciate it that you agreed to go."

"I'm fine," Jenny said, giving her mother's hand a squeeze. "We'll enjoy ourselves today."

"Yes, for today. Then it's work and sacrifice. I know what I have to do."

"Let's get this show on the road." Jenny grabbed her car keys from the small hall table and opened the door for her mother.

"I could drive if you want me to."

"That's okay, Mom." She smiled. As an afterthought she said, "At least the car is paid off."

Her mother's face fell.

"Mom, I'm sorry I said that. Let's just go and forget our troubles for a few hours."

* * * *

When they arrived at the Rowans' sprawling farm, there were several expensive cars in the driveway including Adam's Lexus. She pulled up behind it and turned off the engine. The house and grounds were well kept. The barns in the background were painted white and red to match the sprawling ranch house.

Her mother knocked on the door that was immediately opened by Jack Rowan. He stood in the doorway with a broad smile that lit up his face. He was a rugged-looking man—well over six feet tall with a thick head of gray hair. Age had been good to him. The boys had gotten their height and good looks from him. If she remembered correctly, his wife, Abigail, was a petite little thing with golden-blonde hair she had worn long and straight. Her mother, tall like herself, was almost able to look him in the eye.

She had always hated that she inherited her mother's height. At five foot ten, she had never been considered cutesy like April Mathews who stood maybe five feet in her stocking feet with breasts as large as watermelons. Hers were large, but nothing like April's. Stop it, she told herself. Why did she always feel the need to compare herself with a woman that had always made her feel in some way that she had gotten the short end of the stick.

Jack gave her mother a warm hug and then turned his attention to Jenny. "Oh my, you have grown up since I saw you last," he said with a smile. Turning back to her mother, he said, "You have a beautiful daughter."

"Thank you. She's the light of my life. I can't tell you how glad I am that she's home."

"The boys were both quite taken with your daughter when she went out dancing with them the other night." Directing his gaze to Jenny, he said, "I don't think any of us have seen you since high school."

"You're probably right," Jenny said. "It's been a long time."

"Well, you're here now, and we're happy to have you. Astrid has set the table, and the meal is just about ready."

Astrid, the housekeeper and cook, was still with them. *She must be getting up there in years.*

"Let's go into the living room," he said, ushering them inside the house. "The boys are showing their cousin, Justin, the barns out back. He's in construction and is going to be doing some work for us. You met him before, haven't you, Marlene?"

Her mother sat down on the sofa next to Jack. Jenny sat in the love seat across from them. It was a homey room with throw pillows and afghans flung over the sofas and chairs. There was a brick fireplace with a mantel full of pictures of his sons and wife.

"I have met him before. If I remember right, there's a strong resemblance to your boys."

"Yes. He's Abigail's sister's boy. They live outside of Chicago. Luckily our boys got their looks from the Jones side of the family," he joked.

"They are a reflection of both of you, just like Jenny is of me and Carl. I like to think she got the best of both of us."

"I would say she did," he said, giving Jenny a smile. "But what's this I hear about you not going back to school?"

Not again, Jenny thought, wishing she had never told Luke. It seemed like this was going to be everyone's favorite topic of conversation and not one that she wanted to have to explain over and over again. Her mother spoke up before she could respond.

"Jenny and I talked about it and she has her reasons. I support her and will be happy to have her home. Now tell me what's on the menu tonight. Astrid never ceases to impress me with her cooking skills."

Jack Rowan sat back on the sofa, and although she knew he would have liked to ask her more pointed questions about her decision, he took her mother's lead and let the subject drop.

"Well, for one, she made her famous apple pies for desert."

Jenny loved apple pie and it was common knowledge throughout Brilliance that Astrid Smith's pies were to die for. She smiled.

"She's added a nice filet mignon and a pumpkin spice soup to that along with her scalloped potatoes and fresh green beans. I think you'll be pleased."

"That sounds delicious," Jenny said. "I remember her chocolate chip cookies when I was little. She used to bring them out for your patients. My dad used to come here for his allergy shots, and I loved to come with him just for the cookies. They were so good."

"Better than mine?" her mother asked, making a hurt face, before she laughed. "You don't have to answer that."

Jack was telling her mother about a concert in town the next week when the sound of Luke's voice carried to them from the front of the house. He walked in flanked by Adam and another man that must be their cousin, Justin. Her mother had been right. There was a strong family resemblance. He was gorgeous. He had Luke's dark brown hair and coloring. He also had the same dimple in his chin. But he had Justin's smile.

They were laughing as they walked in the room. Upon seeing her and her mother, they got quiet. She felt the heat of their gazes burning a hole through her. She looked down self-consciously to make sure she hadn't missed a button. When she looked back up, they were still staring at her.

If Jack and her mother noticed the way his sons and their cousin were looking at her, they acted like they didn't.

"Come on in, boys, and say hello to Marlene and Jenny."

Adam and Luke went to her mother first and gave her a kiss on the cheek. She reached up to give each a hug.

"Justin," her mother said, "how are you? It's so good see you."

"It's nice to see you too, Mrs. Clayton. It's been a while."

"That it has," she said, turning to Jenny. "You haven't met my daughter, Jenny. Jenny, this is Justin Morris."

He walked over to where she was sitting and held out his hand. She placed her hand in his, feeling the strength of his grip. When he let go, he sat down beside her. "We're neighbors you know."

"No. I didn't know that," she said, feeling suddenly shy.

"I've moved into the old Hampton place down the road from you and your mom. I have an option to buy."

"So you plan to live here in Brilliance?" Marlene asked.

"I think so. There's work here, and I've been thinking of expanding my business."

"You must be doing well," her mother said.

"He's a go-getter, that Justin," Jack said proudly, as if he were talking about one of his own sons. "He's got a smart head on him for business. He'll do well here."

Jenny knew she should say something. "Welcome to the neighborhood."

"Thank you. I'm sure we'll be seeing each other. I've got an open invitation to Saturday dinners here. From what I've been told, you and your mom do, too."

Jenny just smiled. She wasn't about to open that can of worms. She had promised her mother she would keep the conversation light, and she meant to keep that promise. Justin would find out soon enough that this was the last Saturday dinner her mother and she would be attending at Jack Rowan's dinner table. She saw the slight frown on her mother's face. She knew she was thinking the same thing.

Luke and Adam sat down in a couple side chairs, stretching out their long legs.

"How'd you feel this morning after dancing the night away?" Luke asked, his eyes dipping to her crossed legs.

"I was a bit sore, but I've recovered," she said, tugging her dress down over her knees. She saw the glint in his eye that said he knew he had made her uncomfortable.

"Well, for someone who hasn't danced in a while, you sure tore up the dance floor. You impressed me, and that's not an easy thing to do," Adam said with a laugh that made his eyes twinkle somewhat dangerously.

She felt herself tremble slightly. "I'm glad I passed muster."

"Oh, I would say you more than passed," Luke said.

"You like to dance?" Justin asked, turning his body toward hers.

"It's fun. I'm a bit out of practice. I could barely keep up with them and their friend April." She bit her lip. Why did she have to bring her up?

"April Mathews?" Jack asked, looking at his sons. "I haven't seen that girl in I can't remember when. She still work with her mother as a hairdresser?"

"Yes, she does," Luke said. "She's part owner now. They not only do hair, but all sorts of things like feet and nails and I think massages."

"He means pedicures and manicures," Adam interjected.

"Thanks for clearing that up, Adam," Luke said, giving his brother a mock glare. "Adam has always felt like he has to be my translator."

"Well, someone has to." Adam smiled back at his brother.

"I can you tell that Millie, April's mother, really does a nice job. I go there myself for the works. Next time you need your hair done, we'll go there and get pampered," her mother said to Jenny.

"Sure." There was no way she was going to have April do her hair. God knows what she'd look like when she walked out of the place. Besides that, they didn't have the money for pampering.

Astrid walked into the room. She was slightly hunched over. "Dinner is ready," she said, looking at Jack.

"Thank you, Astrid," Jack said. "I've been thinking about your dinner all day."

"We all have," Luke said, getting up and taking Astrid's arm.

The old woman smiled up at Luke. "I know how much you love a good steak. And there's apple pie for dessert."

"My absolute favorite," Luke said loudly. "Now you all know why I had that gym put in the basement."

"Now you don't need to worry about your weight. You're perfect," Astrid said with a laugh.

"Not that I'm complaining. I wouldn't have it any other way. The only reason Adam and I came here to practice medicine was because we knew you'd feed us."

The older woman was beaming under his praise. Jenny saw real tenderness in his eyes as he affectionately looked down at the older woman. Well, this was a side of Luke she hadn't seen the other night.

Everyone followed them into the dining room. Justin held out his arm for her. He was quite the gentleman. Smiling, she walked with him behind her mother and Jack.

Before they were seated, Astrid excused herself. "I'm tired and I think I'll take a nap. Cassie's going to take it from here."

Jenny had wondered how Astrid was going to do the dinner. She was thinking that she would help her, but that didn't seem necessary now.

When Astrid was out of earshot, Jack said to Jenny, "She's been retired for years, but she still insists on making Saturday dinner. We make sure she has plenty of help. I wouldn't want you to think we were taking advantage of her."

"Oh, no. I think it's wonderful that you kept her on. It's obvious that she loves you all."

"And we love her," Adam said, leaning in Jenny's direction.

"Now don't be shy about eating your fill," Luke said, his eyes resting on Jenny. "Since you've recovered so well from the other night, we thought we'd take you out again. Saturday dances at the Raven's Cove is a great way to work off dinner."

"That's a good idea," Jack said, his eyes meeting her mother's. Her mother looked away, reaching for her water glass.

Jenny wasn't blind. She knew Jack was planning to be alone with her mother and Luke was all for making sure they had the opportunity. She had no intention of going out dancing again, especially after the way Luke had spoken to her before she had shut the door in his face. She felt her face flush slightly. When she looked up from her plate, both Adam and Luke were staring at her with sly grins on their face. They knew exactly what she was thinking.

If it hadn't been unladylike and she wasn't in the company of their father and her mother, she swore she would have stuck her tongue out at them. Instead, she turned to Justin, who she realized was also staring at her, and said with a slightly flirtatious edge to her voice, "I want to hear all about your construction business. Jack seems to think you're quite the businessman."

Justin smiled a lazy smile that told her he knew exactly why she was suddenly interested in his business. He had read Luke's and Adam's expressions and knew she was using him to get to them.

"And there's nothing I want more than to tell you all about the man behind the business. I think you'll find that Luke, Adam, and I are very much alike."

His sultry tone and the way he leaned into her implied a sexual awareness that she had not noticed before. This one was every bit as handsome and dangerous as his cousins. Suddenly, she was all ears. He may not technically be a Rowan, but there was something about him that told her he wasn't kidding when he said that he and his cousins were three of a kind.

Chapter Five

Again, she saw a look pass between him and her mother. This might be her mother's last night with the man. Could she really be heartless enough to ask her to give it up? Dinner passed quickly with everyone raving about the food. Justin kept her entertained with funny stories about growing up with Luke and Adam. It seemed Luke was the instigator even back then and had gotten them all into trouble on more than one occasion.

"Now, you're not painting a very favorable picture of me," Luke had said at one point.

"Hell, I'm not even telling her the real good stuff," Justin shot back. "Unless you want me to?"

"No, I think Jenny's heard enough for one sitting. Let's save some stories for the next dinner."

For some reason, she was really enjoying their stories. She was just glad neither Luke nor Adam had brought up the story of how they had tried to examine her when she was six years old. Her father had brought her with him to the office. She had been sitting in the waiting room when the boys had run in for a cookie and saw her sitting there. She remembered them telling her to come out and play. They had taken her out back of the house and taken her clothes off and just stared at her before they started asking her questions about how she felt and argued about which one of them should test her reflexes. Her mother had been right. They had just been curious and meant no harm.

Her father and Jack had found them. She remembered a lot of yelling. Jack assured her father they wouldn't be examining anyone else in the near future. Both boys had been made to apologize, and that, as far as she was concerned, had been the end of it. However, her father had never seemed too fond of them.

Bringing her mind back to the present, she had to admit, Astrid's cooking was every bit as good as she had anticipated. The steak melted in her mouth. The two apple pies that were for dessert had been eaten with gusto. She had said just a small slice, but with a look from Luke, Cassie had cut her a rather large piece.

"You would have just asked for another piece," he said, catching her glare.

She wouldn't have, but she wanted to. The crust was light and flakey and the apples tasted of cinnamon and sugar with a hint of something else. When she had put the last forkful in her mouth, she sat back and sighed.

Her mother looked over at her. "You enjoyed that. It's good to see you eat." Turning to Jack, she said, "She barely eats at home, just picks, except, that is, when I make my garlic mashed potatoes."

"You do make the best garlic mashed potatoes ever. Daddy used to make you whip up a double batch just so he could eat the leftovers by himself," she said, forgetting for a moment that she was sitting at her mother's boyfriend's dinner table.

"Your father always bragged about them as well as about you and your mother. He was a good man. I know how much you miss him. We miss my Abigail, too."

For the second time that day, she felt tears threatening to spill down her cheeks. She watched her mother reach over and squeeze Jack's hand. There were tears in her eyes, too.

"Well, I'd say it's time we took our coffee out back on the deck," Luke said, breaking the heavy silence. "The ducks are swimming around the pond, and the sun's about to set."

"Good idea," Jack said, rising to his feet. He helped her mother from her chair.

Once they were all seated on the outside deck, she made herself yawn. "I think I'm going to have to pass on the dancing tonight," she said. "I'm actually getting sleepy."

"Oh, no," Luke said quickly. "You need to go dancing. You don't want all that food sitting in your stomach. Trust the doctor to know what's best for you."

"I second that," Adam said. "We're only concerned for your health."

"I'm not a doctor," Justin said, "but if I continue to sit here much longer without moving around, I think I'm going to gain at least ten pounds."

Her mother glanced over at her. She knew what her mother wanted her to do. If she didn't go dancing, her mother would feel obligated to go home with her. And that would certainly put a wrench in Jack's plans for the evening.

"Now, if you are that tired and you're not up for going out," her mother began, "we can go."

"Of course," Jack agreed. "Don't let these boys bully you into going out if you don't want to."

Even if he was the reason for her mother's fall from grace? But in his defense, he didn't know that.

All eyes were on her. "Okay, but I don't want to stay out real late."

"Not a problem," Luke said. "Whatever it takes."

Jenny could read the unfinished sentence in his eyes. *Whatever it takes to get you out of here so our parents can be alone.*

* * * *

The Raven's Cove was in the next town. It had taken them a good forty-five minutes to get there. Adam drove the Lexus. She and Justin sat in the back, however, Luke and Adam kept the conversation going between all four of them. Justin didn't relay any more stories of their childhood. He mostly talked about the house he was renting. He invited her to come over for a visit.

"I could use a woman's perspective," he said. "It's a little rundown, but I think it has possibilities."

"We'll see," she had said noncommittally. The last thing she wanted was to get too friendly with their cousin. She had a feeling that Justin would have liked nothing better. He was sitting a little too close to her, and his arm had sneaked over the back of the seat. He wasn't touching her, but it was a level of intimacy she wasn't sure she entirely liked, although she had to admit she was attracted to him.

The fact was, she was attracted to all three of them. The thought crossed her mind that part of the reason for Justin's move to Brilliance could be because they wanted a woman they could enjoy together. She had no doubt that April would be up for it once she met their handsome cousin if she hadn't already. Why did that thought bother her? It shouldn't. She had no reason to be jealous of April's relationship with any of them. She wasn't vying for their attention. The only reason she was in their company now was because of her mother's relationship with their father.

Once they started dancing, she was glad she had relented to come out with them. Justin was every bit as good a dancer as his cousins. When Luke ordered beers for the table, she was glad to have it to drown her thirst. The beers were going down all too easily between the band's sets. By the end of the evening, she was feeling a little tipsy.

"You want another beer?" Luke asked, looking at her empty bottle.

"No, I think I've had enough. This was fun."

"I told you the doctor knows best," he said, taking her hand. She started to pull away, but he held it firmly. "Let's see," he said, turning her hand palm up. "I'm not a palm reader, but you can tell a lot about a person by their hand."

"Did they teach you that in med school?" she asked.

"No. I learned this technique from a friend of mine. She's into future-telling kind of stuff."

"He means," Adam said, leaning across the table to grab her other hand, "Alisha's into holistic medicine. I think we were peeing green tea for months." He ended with a laugh that made her laugh, too.

"You see this line," he said, pointing to her palm, "that one means you're stubborn, and this one," he continued, "means you're very sensual. I think I got that line, too."

She took her hand back. "You're quacks," she said with a giggle.

"Quacks," both Adam and Luke said in unison.

Justin joined in. "It was only a matter of time before the truth came out."

"Damn, and here we thought our secret was safe," Luke said.

"Speaking of secrets," Jenny said, looking directly at Luke, "Why haven't you told your father you're seeing April Mathews? According to her, you guys are practically married." As soon as she said it, she wanted to take it back. It was a bitchy thing to say. If there had been a hole somewhere, she would have dove into it.

"Should you tell her or should I?" Adam asked.

"Tell me what?"

"You've ruined us for all other women," Luke said with mock seriousness.

"It was seeing you naked," Adam added.

"Whoa there," Justin all but shouted. "You've seen her without her clothes on?"

"You know, Adam...I'm beginning to think you're as bad as Luke," Jenny said, glaring between the two men.

"When did this happen?" Justin asked.

"When I was maybe six," Jenny said, grabbing her bottle of beer. She took a long swig.

"That's why your father hated us, you know," Adam said. "Well, maybe he didn't hate us, but whenever we ran into him, we both got the feeling he didn't want us anywhere near you."

"We were just kids."

"Kids or not, we pretty much knew that you were off-limits," Luke answered.

"But she's not off-limits anymore, right?" Justin asked with a big smile on his face. "I mean, seeing her without her clothes now might inspire me to be a doctor."

"Don't go there, Justin," Luke warned.

"Okay," Jenny said, thinking this would be a good place to end the night. "It's time for me to go home."

"Sorry, Jenny. I was just teasing you," Justin said. "Don't run away."

"I'm not. It really is time to go."

She was surprised there was no argument. Justin picked up their tab, and they left the Raven's Cove without delay. Once again, she and Justin sat in the backseat together. No one said much. It was a quiet ride. They were approaching her street when Justin suddenly turned to her.

"I know you're tired, but I'd love it if you came over to see my place. It isn't that late. How about it? I promise I'll watch my mouth and you don't have to stay that long."

He was looking back at her expectantly. She knew it was a bad idea, but he pleaded so nicely. His dark hair was even longer than Luke's and hung down into his eyes that were magnetic. Powerless to look away, he seemed to be willing her to say what he wanted to hear.

"Okay. But just for a few minutes."

His smile widened to show even, white teeth. She was glad she had made him happy. It was such a little thing to see his place, and it would most likely be her only chance. He would probably blame her, too, when her mother broke up with his Uncle Jack.

"You two okay with that?" he yelled toward the front of the car, not breaking his gaze with her.

"Whatever Jenny wants," Adam began.

"Jenny gets," Luke finished.

Chapter Six

Justin opened the door and turned on the hall light. The house was old and in need of repair. The wooden floors held no shine, and many of the outlets had been pulled. The furniture was new, but everything else, from the faded wallpaper to the worn drapes looked like they had seen better days. There was a toolbox sitting on the one of the steps that led to the upstairs.

"It does need work," he said. "It's going to take time. However, before I get into the heavy stuff, I want to be sure that I'm settling here."

"Well, the place has a lot of potential," Jenny said kindly.

"I think so," Justin said with a smile. "Come and sit down. The sofa is new and clean."

"Holy shit," Luke said, looking around. "Maybe you should be staying with us until you get this place fixed up a bit. Looks like something out of a horror movie."

"Now, it doesn't look that bad," Adam said. "Jenny's right. It has a lot of potential."

"After that remark," Justin said, giving Luke a look of disgust, "I'm not sure I even want to show you the kitchen."

Jenny was about to sit down on the sofa, when she stopped herself. "I want to see the kitchen."

The three of them followed Justin down the hall and into what had one time probably been a very workable kitchen. Now the sink was rusty, and the stove didn't even look like it worked. The refrigerator was one of the small ones that people used for their offices. The cupboards for the most part had no doors, and the counters were stained.

"Okay, I stand corrected," Luke joked. "It's beautiful."

Justin laughed. "I know, it's a mess. But for now, it's all I've got."

"It's good you're in construction," Adam said.

"Construction." Luke all but hooted. "I think demolition is what this place needs."

"If I buy it, I'm getting it pretty cheap. I'll have the money to fix it up."

"They should pay you to take it," Luke said. "However, if anyone can make this place look great, it's you, Justin."

"Why thank you, Luke. Did you just give me a compliment?"

"I think he did," Jenny said, walking over to the sink and looking out the window that was above it. It was dark, but for a small outdoor light. She could see it had a nice big backyard.

Justin walked over and stood behind her. "Your mother told me she had a few things she needed fixing. I'd be glad to help her out. I wouldn't charge."

"Did she? I think the house is fine. But regardless, we don't do freebies."

"Hell, we're practically family," he said, taking a step closer. "Families help each other."

"Well, we're not family…yet," she added, not wanting to sound too severe. "So, let's keep it business for now."

"I've got a few beers in the frig," Justin said, taking a step back.

"I'll have one," Luke said from behind them.

"Me, too," Adam said going to the small frig to help himself. He pulled out four bottles. "One for you, too, Jenny?" he asked, looking her way.

"Sure."

They wandered back into the living room and sat down. She found herself between Luke and Adam. Justin sat in the chair across from them.

"What are your plans now that you're staying home, Jenny?" Luke asked, reaching for her bottle and twisting off the cap.

"Thanks," she said before she took a sip. "Get a job and make some money."

"Doing what?" You said something about helping out your mother? I thought maybe you were going into the real estate business with her?"

She wished Luke would stop with the questions. She should have just gone home and put an end to the evening. Now she had all three of them staring at her like she had three heads. None of them, including their father, liked the idea that she wasn't going back to school. She had a feeling they suspected something was going on that neither she nor her mother was telling them.

"Look, I know you all think it's a mistake that I'm not going back to school. Why you care, I have no idea. But for the record, I'm not going back because I don't want to. Sometimes you need a break and the comment about my mom needing help…well, she's my mom, and I've been away from her too long as Adam pointed out to me the other night. And to be honest, she's still not over my dad's death."

"It's been awhile, and from what I've seen," Adam said, reaching for Jenny's hand, "she seems to be coping with it okay, and I think my Dad's helped. I know she's helped him."

"That's nice," Jenny said, knowing she was treading on dangerous ground. "But things aren't always what they seem. You'll just have to trust me on that one."

"Are you against her marrying our father?" Adam asked, still holding her hand.

"I don't think she's ready to marry anyone."

Justin leaned closer to them. "And what about you, Jenny, are you seeing anyone?"

Although she was happy to take the conversation in another direction, she wasn't about to discuss her sex life with them. "No. I'm not seeing anyone." She wasn't lying. She hadn't been seeing anyone steady since she had broken up with Michael before the end of the previous semester.

He smiled. "I'm glad. Although if you were, it might be easier for you to let your mother go."

"He's right," Adam said.

She realized Adam was still holding her hand. She slipped it out from his. "One has nothing to do with the other. I've never been jealous of your father. That is what you're implying, right?" She was becoming increasingly uncomfortable. She took a gulp of her beer.

"If the shoe fits…" Luke said.

"This conversation is over. You have got to stop interrogating me. I'm tired of it."

"If I thought you were telling the truth, I would," Luke said, putting his beer bottle down on the floor next to the sofa. He turned to her. "What's going on, Jenny? Something doesn't feel right here."

"Oh, so now you're into feelings, is that it? You don't know me. I'm just a kid you knew when we growing up and we weren't friends, and the fact is we're not friends now. The only reason we're here talking is because my mother and your father wanted their *alone* time. Well, they've had it, and now I'm going home."

She got up quickly, too quickly, as her foot snagged Luke's beer bottle and the remaining contents spilled onto the floor. "Damn," she said.

"That's okay. Beer won't hurt these floors," Justin said, getting up to go in the kitchen.

Luke picked up the bottle. "Why are you in such a hurry to get away from us?"

"Honestly. Dancing was fun, but talking with you is something else entirely. It's not fun. What gives you the right to think you can delve into my personal life and that of my mother's? And don't say it's because of your father. They've just been seeing each other. You're taking it a lot more seriously than either of them are, especially my mother."

"You don't think they care for one another? Did you see the way they look at each other?"

Luke had a habit of standing way too close when he was talking to her. She was afraid she was going to lose her balance again. "It's just sex, that's all." She immediately brought her hand to her mouth. She hadn't meant to say that. It sounded so crass.

Luke was looking daggers at her. "If you think it's just sex, you really are immature. And here I thought maybe you had grown up from the spoiled little daddy's girl you once were."

"How dare you talk to me like that. I was never spoiled."

"Hey, you two," Adam said, walking over to stand beside them. "Let's calm it down."

Justin returned with paper towels and started absorbing the spill at their feet. "Could you guys move it over a little?"

Luke grabbed her arm and pulled her away from the sofa. Adam followed. Out of the corner of her eye, she caught a flash of light. She suddenly felt light-headed. She felt her body drifting toward Luke's. She heard him say something before everything went dark.

When she opened her eyes, she was lying on a bed in a room that she couldn't remember ever seeing before. As her eyes adjusted, she saw Luke, Adam, and Justin looking at her from the end of the bed.

"She's awake," Justin said, relief in his voice. "You scared us."

"What happened?" she choked out. Her head was still woozy.

"You fainted. How do you feel?" Adam asked with concern.

She lifted herself on her elbows. "I'm a little weak, but otherwise, I'm fine," she lied. She didn't feel weak at all. What she felt was horny as hell. Waking up from a faint had never made her feel like that before. However, at this very minute, all she could think about was the warmth between her legs that was generating heat at a rapid rate.

"You should lie back and rest for a little while," Luke said, coming over to sit next to her. "You're lucky I was there to catch you."

"Yes, lucky me," she said, looking for her phone, thinking she needed to think about anything but the way she was feeling. "What time is it? My mother's going to be worried."

She saw Luke look over at Justin and Adam before his gaze returned to her. "I called her."

"I wish you hadn't done that."

"I wish you hadn't fainted," Luke said, "but you did."

"If you called her, why isn't she here?" Jenny asked, looking from one man to the other.

"Luke told her you got drunk and passed out here at Justin's," Adam said, shaking his head. "Against, I might add, my better judgment."

"I told her we'd take care of you and bring you home tomorrow."

"Well, that isn't what happened." She looked pointedly at Luke.

"I didn't want to worry her. And," he said, "you *have* been drinking. For all I know you could have had too much to drink."

"Have you seen a doctor lately?" Adam asked from where he sat at the bottom of the bed. "Fainting's not normal. Your blood pressure seems a little low, too."

"You took my blood pressure? That wasn't necessary."

"Has this happened before?" Luke asked, his eyes narrowing.

"I get what's called ocular migraines that cause me to see flickering lights for maybe twenty minutes that I can't get out of my line of vision. Sometimes, not often, but sometimes I faint. It happens quickly and I'm never in pain, and it's not life-threatening according to the doctor at school. He said everyone handles stress differently."

"Are you flunking out of school, Jenny?" Luke took her hand in his. His face had gone from annoyance to what appeared to be real concern.

"No. I'm doing well," she said, enjoying the Luke's touch that was doing strange things to her libido. She didn't want him feeling sorry for her, but the words were out before she could take them back. "They started when my dad died."

Luke squeezed her hand. "I'm sorry. I've been doing nothing but adding to your stress with my talk about your mom and my dad. I had no idea you had anxiety issues."

"I don't have anxiety issues, just something that happens to me once in a while. Nothing to worry about."

"That may be what your doctor at school told you, but I think you owe it to yourself have a complete physical. Also," Adam added, his tone professional, "talking about the death of a loved one to someone trained in that area is pretty normal."

"I'm not a doctor," Justin said, sitting next to Jenny, "but that sounds like real good advice. You're too young to be having migraines."

"I don't think my age has anything to do with it. Like my doctor said, everyone handles stress or maybe I should say, life, differently." Jenny took her hand from Luke's and sat up. "Now, after what you told my mother, I guess she expects me to stay the night."

"I guess she does." Justin laughed. "Lucky for you I just put clean sheets on my bed this morning."

"I'll sleep on the sofa. I'm not taking your bed."

"I want you in my bed," Justin said smoothly. "You're not sleeping on the sofa."

"But where are you going to sleep?" Jenny asked, lowering her eyes.

Justin smiled. "Well, I could sleep with you. But on top of the covers of course. And where Luke and Adam sleep is up to them."

"It's a pretty big bed," Luke said, giving Adam a knowing smile.

"The patient needs her rest," Adam said with a frown. "We should probably just go home."

"I suppose you're right," Luke said, standing up from the bed. "Except I'm not leaving her here alone with Justin."

"Oh, really," Justin said, his eyes resting on Jenny. "And why is that?"

Jenny closed her eyes against her own thoughts. It was a crazy idea and even crazier that she was actually considering letting the three of them curl up in bed with her. She wanted them. Cursing herself for her own weakness, she opened her eyes.

The three of them were staring at her. Slowly, she reached for the buttons on her dress and began to slowly undo one and then the other. She saw Luke's jaw drop. She had worked hard to keep this side of her personality suppressed since she and Michael had split up. He had brought out a wanton side of her that had not only surprised her but made her uncomfortable until he had eased her fears. It still hurt a little when she thought about the end of their relationship. It had been mutual, but nevertheless, it had still been painful.

"Jenny," Luke said, his eyes on her dress that now gaped open to expose her lacy white bra. "As much as I want to, I mean we want to, there's no way I can take advantage of you like this. You're probably still suffering the effects of the migraine."

"Do you really think so, Luke?" she asked, swinging her legs off the bed. Standing in front of him, she continued to unbutton the dress until, with a shrug, it fell off her body. "I feel just fine."

"You look just fine, too," Adam breathed out, his eyes glued to her half-naked body. "You're beautiful, Jenny, but Luke's right. We can't take advantage of you."

"More than beautiful," Justin said from where he still sat on the bed.

She found her courage waning. What if they really didn't want her? What if they were just being nice to her and she had misinterpreted everything?

"Jenny," Adam said, his eyes full of concern and something else that made her shiver. "Are you sure you want us, the three of us?"

She nodded her head, lowering her eyes. "I want all three of you."

"We've all been drinking, and none of us are thinking clearly," Luke said. "We should just leave you to get some rest."

She lifted her head to look up into his eyes that stared back into hers defiantly. Fear and humiliation gripped her. "Don't you want me?" she whispered, her voice wavering, not sure she could bear their rejection.

Chapter Seven

With a groan, Luke hauled her into his arms. "Does this answer your question?"

His lips came down on hers forcefully, his tongue plunging into her softness. His kiss deepened, his tongue swirling in her mouth, causing her to strain even closer to the man she now knew she had never stopped wanting. She moaned back into his mouth as his hands gripped the cheeks of her ass and pushed her into his hardness, rubbing her up against him in sensual movements.

Jenny felt her bra being released. She dropped her arms from around Luke's neck and helped remove the lacy piece of cloth. From behind her, two hands gripped her breasts, kneading them and pulling on her taut nipples. Subconsciously she leaned back. Luke broke their kiss to look down at her breasts that were pale and quivering with desire.

"Her breasts are more than a handful," Justin said, pulling on nipples, his lips raining kisses along her neck.

Adam appeared next to Luke. He leaned down to suck each of her nipples into his mouth. He leaned back and unbuttoned his shirt before he released his belt, unzipping his pants. She almost gasped when he pulled them and his underwear down to reveal his cock that was bigger than any she had ever seen. No one she had ever been with compared to Adam.

Luke pulled his T-shirt over his head before he unbuckled his belt and proceeded to pull his own pants down. This time she knew what to expect, and she wasn't disappointed. His cock was every bit as big as Adam's. Justin's hands slid from her breasts. She knew he was removing his own clothes.

"Take off those panties, Jenny," Luke said, stroking his cock. "Show us your pussy."

On command, she hooked her thumbs in the lacy material and pulled it down over her hips, letting the panties drop to her feet. She stepped out of them, spreading her legs. She had never felt so sexy or naughty. She couldn't explain the intensity of the erotic feelings that were coursing through her like an out-of-control train. She hadn't felt like this since Michael, and even then, her desire hadn't been this overwhelming. All she wanted was to please them with her body. Nothing mattered except the here and now. She wanted all three of them to take her.

Justin's hands snaked around her waist and moved lower. She felt his naked body sliding down her back, his lips on the cheeks of her ass, nipping and biting. His fingers reached between her legs and opened her labia, exposing her clit. She knew she was making mewing noises, but she couldn't help it. She needed their cocks.

Justin tugged on her clit. "Kneel down, Jenny," he said. "Now."

She knelt while his hands continued to manipulate her body. She was now eye level with Luke's cock. She opened her mouth.

"That's a girl, Jenny," Luke said, looking down at her. "Suck my cock, baby."

His cock tasted of soap and sex. She opened her mouth wider, taking him deeper. Justin helped by wrapping his hand in her hair and dragging her head back to open her throat. She craved Luke's cum down her throat.

Luke jerked his cock from her mouth. She looked up, wondering why, when she saw that Adam's cock had replaced Luke's. Smiling, she opened her mouth. Sucking him down her throat, she reached for his balls that were heavy with need. He tasted so good, she wanted more and more. She knew she was acting like a woman possessed, but she didn't care. What did it matter that they knew how much she wanted them? They couldn't hurt her. They were only interested in sex. *So enjoy yourself and don't worry about tomorrow.*

She felt Justin's cock in the crack of her ass. She wasn't unfamiliar with anal sex and had found it to be quite enjoyable with Michael, although he was small compared to these men. Big cocks must run in their family, she thought to herself. No wonder her mother was…She couldn't finish the thought. That was a place she didn't want her mind to go. Luckily, Luke was tired of just watching and said, "Okay, boys. Let's fuck her proper."

"Are you sure, Jenny?" Adam's voice said gently. "We can stop if you want us to."

"Don't stop," she choked out. "Please. I want you."

Adam smiled. "We want you, too, Jenny. Are you ready for us?"

"Yes, I'm ready. I want you all to fuck me. I need your cocks and your cum."

"Damn it, I love it when a woman talks dirty," Luke said, positioning himself underneath her and bringing her pussy down hard on his cock. She loved the feel of his cock inside her. She was more than ready for all of them.

Justin swirled some lube inside her hole. "You like it this way, too, Jenny?"

"Yes. I've never had anyone as big as you take my ass."

"Are you afraid?" he asked, sliding his cock up and down her crack.

"No. I'm not afraid."

"If you want me to stop, I will. Okay?"

"I don't want you to stop. Don't make me beg."

"But you beg so nicely," Justin said, his voice thick with his need.

She felt the head of his cock penetrate her and begin to push. Luke was easing her up and down on his cock slowly. She pushed back into Justin. She wanted more of him. Obliging her, he continued to push through her sphincter muscle until she felt a pop.

He stopped for a few seconds to let her body adjust to his size. Then he began moving back and forth, pushing deeper. There was some pain, but it wasn't long before she felt herself respond to him. Luke, sensing her submission to Justin's cock, began to move her up and down on his cock more forcefully. He and Justin seemed to be totally in tune with one another as they each fucked her, bringing her more and more pleasure with each stroke of their cocks.

"I want to come down your throat, Jenny." Adam's cock was dangling in front of her lips. She wanted nothing more than to have him do exactly that.

"Let me drink your cum," she said, opening her mouth.

Adam groaned as he pushed his cock into her mouth. She had one hand on Luke's chest and one hand now wrapped around Adam's cock. Justin continued to fuck her ass as Luke continued to impale her with his cock, forcing her to ride him harder and harder. It was heaven to be fucked by three men who filled her as deeply as these three. She totally lost control and let out a scream of pleasure when the orgasm that had been building ripped through her. She felt them flowing into all three of her holes.

She had no idea that sex with more than one man could feel this good. The emotions that were lifting her higher and higher were incredible. She was floating somewhere in space and time oblivious to the world before she came back down to earth as their satisfied cocks slipped from inside her, allowing her to crumple onto the bed, their cum dripping from her body.

When she opened her eyes, she smiled. Adam was sitting on the side of the bed and Luke was lying beside her. She suckled and milked Luke as Adam watched. She continued to clean him with her tongue. Justin had left them to go to the bathroom. When he returned, he smiled. "Now, if this isn't a beautiful sight."

"Come here," she beckoned. "Let me taste you, too, now that you're all cleaned up."

Justin did as she asked. She licked him greedily. She couldn't believe she was without any shame as she suckled three men who wanted nothing from her but sex. And yet it all felt so right.

"I knew that mouth of yours could be used for better things than arguing with us," Luke observed. "You know how to give a man what he wants. You've obviously been learning more than just art history at school."

She knew he was fishing. He wanted to know how many men she had been with. That was more like the Luke she had come to know these last few days.

"A lady has her secrets," Adam said, lying across the bed. "Be a gentleman."

"That's okay," she said, removing her mouth from around Justin's semisoft cock that she knew would be hard again if she continued sucking him. "I'm not that experienced, but I'm a quick study. I only had one relationship that was serious."

"You're kidding," Justin said in surprise.

"It's the truth. I wouldn't lie to you."

"I know that. I didn't mean to imply you would. It was meant as a compliment. You're an awesome lover, Jenny."

Jenny righted herself, basking in his praise. "I need a shower."

Luke picked her up before she could protest and took her into the bathroom. Adam turned on the shower.

"I'm capable of showering myself." She tried to move, but Luke held her firmly in his arms.

"No doubt you're capable of a lot of things," Luke said with a smile. "Just relax. Let us pamper you. You deserve it after how well you just took care of us."

The shower was more erotic than she could have imagined. She relaxed and let them soap her body. All four of them were crammed into the small shower stall. They each took turns washing her while they continued to devote their attention to her pussy, breasts, nipples, and ass. She lost herself in their hands that caressed her at the same time. She couldn't believe how easily they made her ready for them all over again.

They had barely dried her off when Justin carried her back to the bed. "Have you ever played with sex toys?" he asked, running his hands over her nipples.

"Sex toys?"

"Don't tell me you don't own a vibrator?"

"No. Well…" She did have one, but that wasn't something she had ever discussed with anyone.

"You do, don't you?" Adam asked with a twinkle in his eye. "There's nothing wrong with that."

"It's for sore muscles, too," she added.

"Well, I've got a muscle that's sore for you," Luke said, standing beside Adam and Justin. "But first, let's try these on those nipples."

She saw Luke open his hand to reveal two regular clothespins. She was confused. "What are those for?"

"Do you want to please us?" Luke asked.

"Yes." She did want to please them.

"I want to attach a clothespin to each of your nipples. It will hurt in the beginning, but it will make your nipples ultrasensitive, and when I remove them, your nubs will ache while I soothe them with my tongue."

Jenny found herself holding her breath, totally consumed by what Justin had just told her he wanted to do to her. Her body seemed to embrace the idea while her mind questioned where this type of play would lead. She couldn't deny that she wanted to find out.

Justin pulled on her nipples, stretching them outward. Jenny watched, fascinated as Luke clamped a clothespin down on each nipple. The immediate pressure on her nipples made her gasp.

"It hurts," she whimpered.

"I know," Justin said, cupping his hand over her pussy before he began to finger her. "You're so fucking wet. Your nipples were made for this kind of sweet torture."

"Now close your eyes while we enjoy your body with our hands and our mouths," Adam said ever so sweetly, making his command sound like a request.

She lowered her eyelids and willed herself to stay calm. Her mind and body were totally and completely in their control. She had never experienced anything so erotic. She shivered slightly.

"Spread your legs, Jenny," Luke ordered.

* * * *

She opened her legs wide upon his command. Luke felt his cock jump. This, he thought, willing himself to slow his passion, was not how he imagined the evening would end. How she had succumbed to their demands so easily astounded him.

He continued to look down at Jenny Clayton's beautiful, naked body. Dark pink areolas the size of half-dollars were in stark contrast to the pale and silky skin of her large, firm breasts. Long dark-auburn strands of hair partially covered her face and shoulders. Although her eyes were closed, her mouth was slightly open. She was magnificent, and for the moment she was theirs to enjoy.

"Good girl, Jenny. Now open them a little wider and touch your clit for me."

He watched her finger open her labia and stroke her clit. He swallowed and looked over to see Adam and Justin were both holding their cocks. By the look on their faces, they were as taken with her as he was. Damn, why did she have to be so fucking perfect? It wasn't like he hadn't been with beautiful women before, but her beauty went deep, and with just a look she could cut right through his defenses. There was something vulnerable and yet so fiercely independent about her that he didn't know whether he wanted to protect her or spank her. She made him want to bury himself deep within her until she begged him for release, while at the same time he wanted to punish her for being a stubborn and willful child.

He thought back on when he had first seen her at the bar. He hadn't believed his eyes when he had glanced over toward the bar and there she was nursing a beer. Her hair had grown, but he still recognized her. Her beautiful mane of dark-auburn hair hung in waves down her back and her body had filled out real nice. When she turned to the bartender who looked like he wanted to scoop her up and eat her, his eyes were drawn to the curve of her neck, her full lips, and those long thick lashes.

At first he was going to ignore her and wait to speak to her another time, but hell, why not, he had thought to himself, she's practically family, and her mother would be pleased that he had made an effort to reconnect with her daughter. Well, maybe reconnect wasn't exactly the right term. Her father had made sure he and Adam were never alone in her company long enough to connect on any level. At parties and community events, whenever they had approached her, he had never been far behind. His protectiveness had increased their level of discomfort to the point they found themselves avoiding Jenny.

Maybe it was knowing that she was forbidden to them or possibly it was just hormones, but she was on their mind a lot during their senior year in high school. When her mother had approached their father about the two of them taking Jenny to a dance, they had been more than willing to escort her. However, the very next day, the dance was off. Jenny told her mother she wasn't going. Or, they had both wondered, had her father got wind of it and put his foot down?

Regardless of the past, she was here now and lying spread-eagled on Justin's bed fingering herself for their pleasure. Her long auburn curls were splayed against the white pillowcase, her skin shiny with a thin layer of perspiration. Reaching down, he squeezed the clothespin on her left nipple. Her eyes flew open. She looked into his, her desire matching his own.

"Do you wish to please us, Jenny?"

She nodded before she brought her finger to her mouth to taste her own juices. Adam and Justin both groaned at the same time. He watched them quickly lie down on her either side of her, using their fingers to tease her clit and caress her breasts. Her gaze never wavered from his while the two men continued to touch her with their hands and now mouths. She arched her back slightly.

"Tell me what you want me to do," she whispered.

Luke smiled. "Bring her downstairs."

Adam and Justin sat up, bringing her with them. He walked ahead of them and down the stairs. He turned to see that Adam held Jenny in his arms. She had her arms wrapped around his brother's neck. Luke could see the imprint of Adam's hand on her hip. Her skin was pale and obviously sensitive. How he ached to make his own imprint on her beautiful body.

Chapter Eight

Jenny clung to Adam, who held her close. She shivered with anticipation of what Luke had planned for her. Her pussy was so hot and her thighs slick with her own juices. She needed to feel them inside her again. She moaned into Adam's hairless chest, licking his nipple. She felt his lips in her hair. She never wanted this night to end, and with good reason. She didn't want to think about how hard it was going to be to not see them like this again. If she hadn't had such a crush on Adam and Luke in high school, maybe she wouldn't have felt such an overwhelming desire for them now. Their cousin Justin was icing on the cake.

"Tie her hands behind her back and then blindfold her," Luke ordered as they entered the living room.

Adam slid her body down his until her feet touched the floor. Justin grabbed her hands and brought them behind her back where he proceeded to tie them with a piece of cloth. Both men led her to a chair where she sat down.

She looked up at Luke, who was watching her intently. Sitting naked before him like this was beyond any type of sexual foreplay she had ever experienced. She wanted the three men to see her like this, her body open and ready for them. She spread her legs and leaned against the back of the chair.

"Do you trust us, Jenny?" Luke asked. He stood in front of her. She couldn't help but let her eyes drop from his eyes to his cock that was erect and so close to her. If her hands weren't tied, she would have reached out to touch to it. Instead, she subconsciously licked her lips.

"Yes, I trust you," she said, willing her eyes upward until she was looking into eyes his once again.

"There are a variety of ways to bring a woman to orgasm. Some more obvious than others," he said, his hand reaching out to lightly caress her breasts and pull on the clothespins that secured her sore nipples. She ached to be more than just touched.

She couldn't control her sigh of desire as his fingers lightly traced her areolas. She tested her restraints. Her fingers longed to touch him, but he had taken away her ability to do so. It was torture of the sweetest kind.

She glanced over at Adam, who was sitting on a chair, his legs wide and his cock pointing in her direction. Justin was every bit as handsome, and his cock matched theirs. They were magnificent men, exceptional in every way.

"Justin," Luke said, nodding to where his cousin stood watching them, his hard, muscled body leaning in her direction. "Blindfold her."

"What?" she asked, her eyes flying to Luke's. "I want to be able to see you."

"I know." Luke smiled. "And I want to increase your every sense until you know your body as well we intend to. The true measure of sexual fulfillment is the art of self-control coupled with desire born from trust of the unknown."

Jenny sat still as Justin covered her eyes and tied the blindfold behind her head. She felt a slight shiver of apprehension when she felt him back away from her. Luke was in charge. There was no doubt about that. Adam and Justin both seemed quite content to let him give the orders. However, she knew they weren't weak. She waited in silence. Minutes went by, and there was no sound except for her breathing. Had they left her? She would have heard them. Finally, she couldn't stand it any longer.

"Please," she said, "I need you."

"Spread your legs wider, Jenny," Luke said, from behind her. She almost jumped. Immediately she opened her legs wider.

"You're beautiful," Adam's voice floated to her from somewhere on her right. "You're so wet. What do you want, Jenny?"

"You," she practically yelled. "I want you all. Don't make me beg."

"Oh, but we like it when you beg, especially when you do so from your need for us," Luke whispered into her ear. "Beg, Jenny, beg like the sweet little slut you are for what you want so desperately."

She trembled uncontrollably. Every nerve ending in her body was on edge. She wanted to be fucked. She had never wanted a man to take her the way she wanted these three men to take her. "I need it. I want it. Please."

"Need what? Want what?" Luke's breath touched her cheek. She strained toward him.

He repeated his questions.

"I need your cocks," she said. When Luke didn't say anything, she continued. "I need them in my mouth, my pussy, and my ass. I need to make you come."

"And what do you want us to do with our cocks?"

"I want you to fuck me," she said, instinctively knowing that they wanted to hear her say the word *fuck*.

"Say it again, our sweet, beautiful little slut."

"Please fuck me. Please. I need you to fuck me."

"Very good, Jenny. Very good."

She felt warm and happy as well as horny. She would do anything if they would just give her what she needed.

"Stand up and bend over the chair so that the clothespins just touch the seat."

"Now."

She felt slightly disoriented. Not sure of herself, she sat back down.

"You're not moving fast enough, Jenny. When I speak, you do as you're told."

"Yes, Sir," she said before she realized she had called him Sir.

She immediately stood up and turned, hoping she was doing it right. She leaned over what she hoped was the chair and lowered herself until the tips of her nipples rubbed against the coarse material of the chair seat. Minutes passed as she waited for their next command. Suddenly she was lifted by strong hands into the air and forced to kneel on the floor.

"Adam's cock needs sucking, Jenny. It's right in front of you."

She felt a slap on her behind that motivated her forward. Evidently Adam was now sitting in the chair she had vacated. She slipped between his open legs and found his cock with her mouth. She kissed his balls and licked them. Moaning softly, she took him into her mouth and suckled him. His cock swelled, filling her mouth full until she started to choke. She gasped for air when he pulled himself from her.

"No," she whimpered. "I want more."

"I know, baby," Adam said, "And you'll have it. A lot more."

Once again she felt a couple slaps on each of her ass cheeks. It burned slightly. She could feel the heat of Luke's hand or what she assumed was Luke's hand even after he had stopped. She wiggled her ass as her pussy contracted in pleasurable spasms. She was so close to coming.

"You are not to come," Luke said sharply.

"But I want to," she cried out.

In response, she received another slap on each of her butt cheeks, but this time harder. She felt tears come to her eyes. Were they displeased with her? However, almost immediately she felt a cool salve being rubbed on each cheek. It felt good.

"Does that feel better?" This time is was Justin who spoke to her and whose hands were massaging her ass.

"Yes, but you spanked me."

"Luke spanked you," Justin said softly. "Your ass is so white that the imprint of his hand is still there. Did he hurt you?"

"A little," she said. "But it felt"—she supposed she should be truthful—"good, too."

She was lifted upward. The cloth was untied from around her hands. She was almost positive it was Luke that had released her. He confirmed it when his lips touched her ear. "It was a simple way of helping you control your desires. A combination of pleasure and pain can open your mind and body to a level of experience beyond anything you can imagine."

Magically it seemed, her blindfold was gone. She opened her eyes and squinted. It took a moment for her eyes to adjust to the light. She was still being held by Luke, who was looking down at her with a smile.

"Luke," she breathed. "I don't know how much more I can stand. My body feels like it is going to burst."

"I think I can speak for the three of us when I tell you that we feel the same way, except we understand the need for patience. You've been so good. You've tried so hard to please us."

Jenny nodded. The clothespins rubbed against Luke's chest. "I want to be good."

"It's time, my sweet, beautiful slut," Luke said, his voice husky and thick with need.

Gently, he released both clothespins. She gasped from the pain as the blood surged back into her sore nubs. Luke took each one into his mouth. Moaning, she pleaded with him to let her come.

He nodded to Adam and Justin, who walked over to where they were standing.

"Fuck her. I want to watch while she orgasms. When you've come inside of her, bring her back to me."

Justin held out his arms. Luke gave her to him. She looked back at Luke who had sat down, his eyes glued to hers. Justin smiled at her and kissed her forehead. "We're going to make you purr like a well-satisfied kitten."

Justin carried her to the sofa. He positioned her above him and brought her down as he pushed upward to impale her on his cock. She slid down his shaft, shuddering from the spasms coursing through her pussy. She almost couldn't breathe from the intensity of the feelings that made her suddenly faint. Luckily, she remained conscious, thinking she couldn't blame her lack of control on a stress migraine. She had never felt so relaxed or so good.

Adam was behind her, his lips on her neck. She strained backward. Justin was cupping her breasts and tugging on her nipples. Adam inserted his finger between her ass cheeks. She could feel the lube as he pushed deeper. She knew his cock would not be far behind.

"Yes," she said, leaning back, her arms reaching behind her to grab him around his neck. Her breasts pushed outward. The head of Adam's cock entered her. She felt his urgency as he pushed deeper and deeper into her tight hole. She cried out as both men's cocks filled her. Moving in unison, the two men fucked her harder and harder until she felt each one of them shudder as they released their cum inside of her. She turned to look at Luke. His eyes were glazed over with desire. She watched as he stroked his cock. He nodded.

"Don't look away from me, Jenny," he said, his voice raspy. "I want to see your face when you come."

She started to shake as the long-awaited orgasm ripped through her. She felt as if he were inside her, too. His eyes willed her to ride each wave of pleasure that flowed through her. She knew he could feel every beat of her heart, every nuance, and every breath she breathed. She watched him jerking himself off. However, something told her he wouldn't come without her.

Justin lifted her body upward and Adam slipped his cock from between the cheeks of her ass. Adam's breath was on her neck. "Go to him, Jenny."

She wanted nothing more than to do just that. She walked to him with cum dripping from her pussy and ass. Nothing mattered except pleasing Luke. She dropped to her knees in front of him. He hauled her onto his lap and kissed her. She lost herself in the kiss that made her pussy contract in spasms all over again. It was all she could do to not come. She knew better. God, how she wanted him.

* * * *

Adam watched his brother kiss Jenny. How was this possible? She was beyond his wildest dreams or expectations. He had thought she would be fun in bed once she got over being so prickly, but he had no idea that she was their perfect match. No woman had ever brought out this side of them on their first night together unless she was a professional. Not that they had need of professionals, but every now and then Luke liked to hire women who could give them more heightened experiences. They had found the best way to do that was with someone who embraced their lifestyle without reservation.

Jenny was better than any of them. Her beautiful ass still dripped his cum as Luke released her and pushed her back down her knees to suck his waiting cock. Her skin was pale and translucent. The cheeks of her ass were plump and still pink from Luke's spanking. He had never seen his brother into a woman the way he was with Jenny. From the moment he had sat down at the bar, Luke had been different. Adam had felt the attraction, but Luke was consumed by it. And now Adam knew why. One night with her, and he was ready to ask her to marry them. However, he knew that tomorrow everything could look different. Besides, this was only their first night together, and having her mother and his father practically married already presented a slight complication and one he was sure had not escaped Luke. It just reinforced their uncontrollable desire for her.

Luke was totally oblivious to them as he pushed his erection deeper into Jenny's mouth. Adam didn't think he would ever tire of seeing Jenny naked and sucking either his, Justin's, or Luke's cock. He loved the way she opened so readily for them and wanted nothing more than to pleasure them with her body. Luke was close to coming. She sucked him faster and harder, her entire body shaking with her efforts. Luke groaned, his head back, his body spasming with each spurt of his cum that Jenny drank. Some of it escaped from the corners of her mouth and dribbled down her chin. It was beautiful to watch.

"Surprised by her?" Justin asked, his own voice thick. He stood naked beside Adam.

"She's amazing."

"I know. Maybe too amazing. Have you ever seen Luke quite like this before? I haven't."

"She's always held an attraction for him, even when we were kids. I think the fact that her father didn't like us much intensified it."

"You don't think it's a one-time thing, do you?"

"I hope not. She's got something special, and I for one want her back in our bed again and again."

"Oh, I do, too. I'm just not entirely sure about her."

"What do you mean?"

"Just a feeling that she's got something going on that we don't know about. Don't ask me why. I just think we should be careful."

"You could be right. I hope you're wrong."

Both men returned their attention to Luke and Jenny. They watched as she licked his cock and drank as much of him as possible. Luke had a big grin on his face.

"Are you ready to get some rest? I'd say it's about time we all got a little sleep," Adam said, looking down at Luke and Jenny.

"Just as soon as our sweet Jenny cleans herself," Luke said, smiling at Jenny.

Jenny scooped cum into her mouth from her pussy and breasts. All three men watched as she cleaned herself. Adam went into the kitchen and returned with a warm cloth that he used to clean whatever cum was left on her body.

When she was clean, Luke carried her upstairs and laid her on Justin's bed. "You know," he whispered in her ear, "that when I call you my sweet slut, it means you please me. Do we please you, Jenny?"

"More than you will ever know," she whispered back before her eyes closed.

Chapter Nine

Justin woke up first and went into the kitchen to put on a pot of coffee. They had debated about sleeping with her but had decided that since not all three of them could fit in the bed, they would all sleep in the living room. Justin knew that if they had been in bed with her, they would have wanted to take her again, and it was probably best that they control their urges where she was concerned.

The thought of her sweet ass, pussy, and mouth already had him hard. She had the power to make them want her without any forethought to the fact that she was practically a stranger to them. Luke and Adam hadn't seen her since high school, and yesterday was the first time he had ever laid eyes on her.

Luke had encouraged him to ask her back to his place because he wanted to find out more about why she was staying in Brilliance and not going back to school. Sex with her had never entered the equation. At least he thought it hadn't. However, he was never entirely sure about Luke's agenda. His cousin had always kept one step ahead of him and Adam.

He poured himself a cup of coffee as Luke entered the kitchen wearing just a pair of jeans. "Good morning, cousin."

"Morning, Justin. I smelled the coffee brewing, and I could sure use a cup."

"Thought you might need one. I guess Adam's still snoring."

"Yup."

Justin poured Luke a cup of the strong liquid and handed it to him. "This will grow hair on your chest."

"I like it strong."

"Good."

"One helluva night, wouldn't you say?" Luke asked, pulling a rickety chair up to the kitchen table that looked more like a workbench. He sat down.

"You're not kidding. I can't get her out of my head."

"We need to be careful with this one," Luke said before he took another sip of his coffee.

"I pretty much said the same thing to Adam," Justin said, leaning against the sink. "When I'm with her, I'm consumed with her. I'm not used to getting so wrapped up in a woman so quick."

"Hell, I knew I wanted her, knew we all did, but it wasn't until after she fainted that I felt a change in her. It was as if she threw all caution to the wind. She wanted us every bit as much as we wanted her."

"I know. She surprised me, too, yet it all seemed so natural. It was like it was meant to happen. It was almost too perfect."

"She scares the shit out you, doesn't she?"

"If I'm scared," Justin answered. "It's the kind of scared I wouldn't mind getting used to. It's just I've never been with anyone I felt so in tune with so quickly. It was like I inhaled and she exhaled. Can't help it if I'm feeling a bit unbalanced."

He was more than just a little unbalanced by what had transpired between them. Just saying her name could make him hard for her. He shook his head and went back for another cup of coffee.

"I felt it, too. So, what do we do now?"

"You tell me." Justin laughed. He had known from before he could remember that his cousin Luke was the alpha male. He and Adam were dominant in their own right, but Luke called the shots. So why was he asking him what to do?

"I always want to know what you think, and because we're so close, I usually do without asking. The same holds true for Adam. However, with Jenny it's different. She makes me question everything I thought I knew. I want her."

Justin smiled. "I think you just answered your own question. Maybe it's time we went to check on our guest."

* * * *

Jenny rolled over into something hard and firm. She snuggled down deeper into the covers. She didn't want to open her eyes. It felt so good to just relax.

From behind her, she felt the covers lift. Within seconds she was wide awake. She gasped as she realized she was sandwiched between two men with very large, very hard cocks pressing into her naked body.

Luke's cock was hard against her stomach. She lifted one leg over his, giving him access to her pussy. Strong hands grabbed her breasts from behind, pulling on her sore nipples. She moaned softly, pushing into Luke's cock.

"So glad you woke up for us, Jenny." Luke smiled into her wide eyes. "I missed you."

Jenny hid her face in Luke's chest as his cock slid inside her. She couldn't believe this was happening again. She should get up and leave, but her body had other ideas. *What am I doing?*

She should have never let them talk her into visiting Justin's, but if she were truthful, she was glad they had. Last night had been incredible in every way. Was that why she had gotten that damned migraine and fainted? Had she somehow known she was destined to be in their bed even when she knew it was more than wrong? She had told her mother to break it off with Jack, and here she was enjoying his sons and nephew in ways that she never thought possible. And the worst part was she was going to let it happen again.

Groaning inwardly, she bit her lip to stifle her cries of need as she felt a cock slide in between her ass cheeks. Nothing mattered but the way they made her feel. She could already distinguish their cocks. It was Justin's that pushed into her tight hole. She was so ready. There was no doubt in her mind that she must have been dreaming about sex. Without words they simply took their pleasure with her. Each stroke took her closer and closer to an explosion of what she knew would be multiple orgasms.

Wrapping her legs around Luke, she lost herself between the two men who continued to fuck her forcefully and without mercy. Her whole body was shaking uncontrollably when they both exploded inside of her. Their warm liquid filled her with an unbelievable sense of well-being that only served to heighten the experience. They had taken her as if she belonged to them. She was still trembling with the aftershocks of the climax that she had felt in her toes when Luke and Justin rolled away from her, allowing her a few moments to try and catch her breath. She dragged the sheet up to cover herself. It would be so easy to forget her problems and to want this to be more than it was or ever could be.

"Good morning, Jenny," Luke said, rising up on one elbow to look down at her. "I don't like it when you cover yourself," he said, yanking on the sheet. "I like you like this. Naked and dripping with our cum."

Jenny lay still as Luke dragged the sheet down until her body was completely exposed to their eyes.

"Good morning, Luke." She turned to smile at Justin. "Good morning, Justin."

"It is a very good morning," Justin said, returning her smile.

"Where's Adam?"

"Still sleeping. He's going to wish he woke up." Luke laughed. "He's always required more sleep than I do."

"I may have to go downstairs and wake him up," Jenny said and then giggled, feeling reckless and carefree. "He was always my favorite twin."

"Is that so?" Luke yelled playfully, cupping her wet pussy. "Looks like I've got my work cut out for me."

"Yes," she said, enjoying the laughter in his eyes. "You certainly do. Think you're up to the task?" *Now why did I say that?*

"I'm surprised you'd even ask after last night and this morning."

"You're right. I shouldn't have asked. In fact, I really should get dressed and go home. My mother will be waiting for me."

"You think she'll be home?"

"Why wouldn't she be?"

"Are you really that naïve or did you forget she spent the night with my father?"

"Oh."

"Oh? Is that all you have to say?"

"All the more reason why I should leave. I don't want her to know about what happened. It's not part of our plan."

"What do you mean, your plan?" Justin asked, confusion in his voice.

Lying there naked made it hard for her to think rationally or logically. Telling them that being in their bed was not part of the plan was just plain stupid. Groaning, she tried to get up, but Luke pushed her back down onto the bed.

"You didn't answer his question," Luke said, all the playfulness gone from his voice.

There was something about Luke when he got serious like this that turned her on like a light switch. It was crazy, but she liked it that he wasn't about to let her get away without explaining herself. It wasn't like her to allow a man to dominate her like this. What, she wondered, would he do if she refused to answer?

"Jenny."

She heard the warning in his voice. It just intensified her need to challenge him further. "I don't have to answer your question. My plans are my business."

Luke stared down at her, his eyes cold, his features like granite. She held her breath. Had she gone too far?

"You know what? You're right. Your plans are none of my business. Justin and I are going to clean up and then we'll leave you to get dressed. When you're ready, I'll take you home."

His anger was like a slap in her face. Jenny watched the two men get off the bed and walk away from her. They were gorgeous, and she wanted them back in bed with her, yet hadn't she been looking for a way out of this? She should be grateful she had made him mad and they were letting her go. Luke had put her in her place, and she would do well to remember that she belonged anywhere but here with them.

It didn't take the two of them long to clean up and get dressed. No words were spoken as they walked out of the room. She got up and stripped the bedsheets that needed to be washed. When she was done, she went into the bathroom and showered. She couldn't help but be reminded of the three men washing her with such care. She moaned. She wanted all three of them again, but that would selfish on her part. She had no intention of pursuing a relationship with them. And, she knew without a doubt, having witnessed Luke's anger when she hadn't answered Justin's question, that when her mother broke it off with Jack, he would be livid by what he would think was her part in their breakup.

Showered and dressed, she walked downstairs. Adam was still asleep in a chair. She couldn't believe he had actually been able to sleep with his legs hanging off the arms of the chair and his body contorted in a position that looked anything but comfortable.

Luke walked out from the kitchen with the keys to the car in his hand. He walked past her and opened the front door. Justin hadn't even come out to say good-bye. She walked past Luke and down the steps to Adam's Lexus. Luke got to the car first and opened the passenger door for her. She slid in.

The drive to her house was thankfully short. She could have walked, but she didn't want to argue with him. When he pulled the car into her driveway, she opened her own door.

"Good-bye, Luke."

"Bye, Jenny."

She knew he was watching her walk up the steps to the porch. She opened the front door without looking back. She closed it behind her before she burst into tears. Looking around for her mother, she quickly got control of her emotions. The last thing she wanted was to have to explain her tears to her mother. However, she soon discovered that her mother wasn't home. Luke had been right. Her mother must have spent the night with Jack and still wasn't home.

Climbing the stairs she went to her room and threw herself across the bed. Her body was still feeling the effects of their lovemaking or what she knew now was simply sex. She got up and stripped off her clothes and touched her nipples that were ultrasensitive. She could see her reflection in the mirror. She still had her need for them written all over her face. Damn them for making her want them.

Chapter Ten

Luke drove back to Justin's in what seemed like seconds flat. He couldn't remember being so angry with a woman before. Jenny had gotten to him in more ways than one. He had thought they would at least spend the rest of the morning enjoying that delicious body of hers and giving her what he thought she wanted. She had seemed so eager to please them last night and then again that morning. But she had plans, and he, Adam, and Justin obviously weren't part of them.

For a moment, he had wanted to physically throttle her, but he was not a man of violence, at least not the kind that resulted from anger. And even then, he had his limits that had been tested with a number of women he had bedded. Some of the more aggressive ones had wanted him to beat them, but that wasn't his style. He enjoyed dominance, it was his nature, but never to the point of causing harm. Jenny was the first woman that had made him see red, and that in itself was enough to tell him his feelings where she was concerned were stronger than they should be. They were practically family already. He had made a mistake with her.

When he walked back through Justin's front door, Adam was standing there waiting for him.

"What the fuck happened?"

"She wanted to go home. Where's Justin?"

"He left a note. Said something about checking on a job."

"Okay. You about ready to go home?"

"No. Not until you tell me why she left without even saying good-bye to me."

Luke shook his head. He knew he had to tell him. He just didn't feel like talking about it now. But when had that ever stopped Adam from hounding him?

"She made it known that she had plans and we weren't a part of them. We had a feeling she was a bit of a bitch, and we were right."

"She's also fucking fantastic in bed. There was no bitch in her last night."

"I guess I brought it out in her this morning, then."

"What did you do, Luke?"

"You were sleeping. Justin and I weren't."

"You can be a real bastard sometimes, especially when you don't get your own way."

"I asked her a simple question, and her answer was that it was none of my business. You can ask Justin when you see him. Fact is, it's probably better this way. It was a mistake to get involved with her."

"That's what I thought. You pushed her, and she pushed back. You two were at odds right from the beginning, but I thought you had gotten past that. Guess I was wrong."

"So did I, but I was wrong, too. I lost it last night. I knew better, but I let my cock think for me. She brought me back to reality this morning."

"I guess it was after you fucked her."

Luke stared hard at Adam. His brother rarely ever got angry, and never about a woman. Adam was the most level-headed person he knew. But the tone of his voice was anything but calm.

"Is that was this is about? You're pissed because we didn't wake you up? It's never bothered you before when Justin and I have enjoyed some morning pussy while you were sleeping."

"I'm not pissed. But you should have woken me up."

"I was wrong to do that. I'm sorry. But believe me when I tell you she's not right for us."

"But damn, if it didn't feel right," Adam said with a sigh. "It's never been like that for the three of us with any woman."

Luke walked toward his brother. "I admit it. But that's not going to change anything. She could have a boyfriend waiting for her back at school for all we know."

"Maybe. But I don't think so."

"Doesn't matter. We're not going to fuck her again, and that's that."

"We've fucked a lot of women, and what happened last night wasn't just a good fuck and you know it."

"Listen, we can talk about this until we're blue in the face, but it won't change the fact that we made a mistake. I'm tired," Luke said. "Let's go home."

"Okay. But I'm not as sure as you are that this is over by a long shot."

"It is for me."

Luke knew how Adam felt, but he couldn't let his own feelings cloud his judgment. Something in her eyes had warned him she wasn't being truthful, and the one thing he hated was dishonesty. Even if she had lied, he knew her body hadn't lied to them. All he needed to do was find someone to fuck in the next few days and they'd all forget about Jenny. At least that was his plan.

When they arrived back at the house, his father wasn't there. He had probably taken Marlene home. Adam went directly upstairs to his room. He had complained the whole way home about what a poor night's sleep he had gotten. As much as they were alike, they had totally different sleeping habits. Adam needed a good eight hours a night, and he on the other hand needed less than five.

He was full of nervous energy and decided to go into town to get something to eat. The café's tables were all occupied, so he opted for a seat at the counter where he ordered a burger and fries. Not the healthiest thing on the menu, but today he didn't care.

The waitress had just placed his plate of food in front of him when April Mathews sat down in the seat next to him. "Hey there, April," he said pleasantly. He liked April, even if she was a bit of a flirt. He knew she wanted more than friendship, but he and Adam both had no desire to pursue what she had offered. He had enough respect for her not to play with her. He also didn't want to hurt Jenny. Too bad he hadn't been able to show that kind of restraint with Jenny. April interrupted his thoughts.

"How come you haven't called me to go out dancing again?"

"Well, if I remember right," he said with a smile, "You called me."

"Now, let's not split hairs," she said jokingly. "You know you've always played hard to get. What was a girl to do?"

"You're a lot of fun, April, and I enjoyed dancing with you. But…"

"No buts," she said, interrupting him. "We enjoy each other's company, and that includes Luke. We should go out more often. You might find that you enjoy more than just dancing with me."

"April…" he warned.

"Don't be such a prig, Luke. I love to dance." She smiled seductively.

"What happened between you and the Landers brothers? When I was home on break a year or so ago, you guys were pretty hot and heavy. Someone said you were engaged to them."

"We broke up a few months ago. They got a wandering eye and I found out about it. Fact is, I caught them practically in bed with that whore, Jillian Palmer."

Luke remembered Jillian Palmer. She was an attractive girl who had developed early and had worn clothes to enhance her assets. According to some of the guys, she had been an easy lay in high school and even before that. He'd heard she worked as a stripper at some club in the next town. Funny, the few times he had contact with her, she hadn't seemed like a bad sort. If anything, she had come across as shy. That, he thought, was obviously just a misconception on his part. "I'm real sorry, April. I really am. That must have been rough."

"They both said it was nothing and that she came on to them, but that didn't make it any better in my eyes," she said, getting teary. She caught herself, blinked, and tried to smile. "I'm a free agent now, and I can do whatever I want with whoever I want."

"Sounds to me like you're still in love with them."

April's face crumpled. "I don't want to be. I need to move on."

"Is that what you really want?"

"Doesn't matter what I want. They betrayed my trust, and I can't be with someone like that."

"Believe me, I understand. But love isn't rational, and it doesn't follow a plan or rules. When you love someone, sometimes you just have to forgive them or at least give them a second chance."

"Guess my confession just put an end to any romance between us." She smiled. "And here I was trying to get you to ask me out and not feel sorry for me."

"We're friends, April. I'm here if you need to talk. Luke's a good listener, too. Believe me when I tell you, we make better friends than lovers."

"I don't believe that for a second," she said softly. "But thanks for your offer of friendship. I appreciate it."

"Why don't you let me buy you lunch?"

"I did come in here to eat. I'm on my break from the salon. But you don't have to buy me lunch."

"It would be my pleasure, if you'd let me."

"Thank you, Luke."

Now I know what was going on with her. He should have asked long before this. Adam had told him he could be self-absorbed at times, but then, he hadn't asked her either. He knew they both had both seen her as just a piece of fluff for fun. Little did they know she was nursing a broken heart.

Why, he wondered again, couldn't they have used more logic when it came to Jenny? He had lost all reason when she had submitted herself to their lust, but Adam and Justin had been just as eager as he had been to sample her body. However, if he had shown more control, they would have followed suit, and he wouldn't be feeling like shit now. He should have never let her get under his skin, especially this morning when she had spoken to him as if he didn't matter. She had caught him off guard, and it hurt. Not something he was used to feeling from a woman. It was usually the other way around.

"Luke?" April asked, touching his arm. "What's wrong?"

"Uh, nothing. Just thinking," he said, forcing a smile. "Now, let's talk about more pleasant things, like the upcoming Summer Festival. It's all the buzz around here, and I was wondering if you and your mom will still have a booth to cut hair for the kids with cancer."

April smiled. "We sure do. And I'm still looking to sign people up. You interested in letting me run my hands through that gorgeous hair of yours?"

They both laughed. It was an easy laugh that felt natural. April understood they could only ever be friends. Was that what Jenny wanted, just to be friends, or did she even want that?

Chapter Eleven

Jenny hadn't realized she had fallen asleep until she was woken by the slamming of the front door. Her mother must be home. She pulled on a pair of sweatpants and a lightweight jersey. She was just about to open her door that was slightly ajar when it was pushed open. Her mother stood in the doorway, tears running down her face.

"What happened?"

"I broke up with Jack," she choked out before she broke into sobs.

"Oh, Mom," Jenny said, wrapping her arms around her mother. "I'm sorry. I know I told you to do it, and I stand by that, but I'm so sorry."

"It had to be done, and I couldn't be with him again. Too painful," her mother whispered, her voice barely audible.

They stood silently for a few minutes, Jenny's arms holding her mother close until she regained her composure.

"It was the hardest thing I've ever done. Jack's hurt and angry, and he doesn't understand why. And I couldn't explain it to him without telling him the truth. I'd rather he hated me than to know what I've done. His anger is better than the rejection and disgust he wouldn't be able to hide."

"He'll never have to know, Mom. I told you that."

"That's what I'm holding on to. I won't let you down. I promise."

"We're going to get through this together, Mom. We just have to stick to the plan. I'm going to map out a budget for us and get a job."

"You could work with me. I mean, together, we could branch out to some of the nearby towns. I know you don't have your real estate license, but you can show houses and I could help with all the settlements."

"It's a thought, but I'm not sure putting all our eggs in one basket is the solution. If your business slows down, we still need to pay the bills and now that there's no backup, we need a second income that's not tied into yours."

"I see your point," her mother said sadly. "I've made such a mess of things."

"You have to stop dwelling on what's happened and concentrate on the future. We can't get bogged down with feeling sorry for ourselves." Jenny knew she wasn't only talking about their financial situation. She had to put what happened last night and this morning out of her head. It was a mistake and it was over. Just like her mother's relationship with Jack, it was best forgotten or at least put away where it couldn't cause any more damage. She and her mother both needed to be strong.

She heard her cell phone ringing and for a moment she thought maybe it was Luke, but that thought was short-lived as she saw her friend Anne's name pop up on her display.

"My friend Anne's calling."

"Go ahead and take the call. I'm exhausted. I think I'll lie down," she said from over her shoulder, already on her way to her own bedroom.

Jenny watched her mother close her bedroom door behind her before she answered her phone. "Hi, Anne?"

"Jenny. I was thinking about you and thought I'd give you a call. Thought maybe we could get together for coffee or something. You know, I'm only twenty minutes away."

"Coffee sounds great. I'm glad you called. I should have called you. How've you been?"

"I got a job for the summer. How about you?"

"Not yet, but I'm glad you did. Where at?"

"The Redrock Casino. I'm a cocktail waitress."

"No kidding."

"And they're still hiring. Think you'd be interested? It's union, so the pay isn't bad and the tips are fantastic."

"I don't know. I mean, I thought I'd find something closer to home. My mom still has my dad's truck in the garage, but I don't know how well it runs, so I could be kind of stuck."

"It's shift work, so that could be a problem because you'll work mostly at night. But if you change your mind, let me know. In the meantime, let's plan to get together. How about this time next week?"

"Okay. Where did you want to meet?"

They talked a few minutes longer. Jenny was going to tell her she wasn't coming back to school but decided it could wait. She didn't feel like discussing it over the phone. She knew Anne would be full of questions, and she wasn't prepared to start lying to her, although she knew it was inevitable.

Jenny spent the rest of the day going over a budget. It looked like if they were to be able to survive without selling the house and declaring bankruptcy, she would need to find something that paid pretty well. The job at the casino would probably pay better than any of the jobs she might be able to get. Fact was, she had no idea where to even look at this point. It was ironic that she would even consider working at the casino. Maybe it was only justice that she get a job making money at the place where her mother had lost all their money.

That night at dinner, she asked her mother about her father's old truck. She would need it, regardless of where she got a job. However, her mother had already been thinking about her transportation.

"Your father loved that old truck. I guess that's why I couldn't bear to part with it. And I also knew you might need it to get around in when you were home from school. And you did use it a few times."

"But how does it run now? That's the question."

"Well, I started it up not long ago because it needed to be inspected. It did cost a few hundred dollars, but the mechanic said it was in good working order. I wouldn't want you to take it on any long trips, but I think it will be fine for local travel."

"You know my friend Anne called."

"Yes. You were talking to her when I took my nap."

"She's working at the casino as a cocktail waitress, and she told me they have openings. From what she says, the money is good."

"You're not actually thinking of working there?" her mother asked. There was not only surprise but dread written all over her face.

"I wouldn't if I thought I could find something that paid well around here. I made a few calls this afternoon and so far, no one is hiring and the pay is minimum wage even with a college degree."

"I was afraid of that," her mother said, before she took a sip of her ice water.

"Anne and I are supposed to meet for coffee later this week, but I'm thinking I'll call her tomorrow about the job. I can use the truck when you're out, but at night, I could use your car just to be on the safe side."

"You're serious?"

"I'm considering it. I mean, I have to get hired first."

"Oh, they'll hire you. The way you look, they'll snatch you up in a second. Those girls that bring you drinks are all young and pretty and they can wear the uniform quite well." Her mother shook her head. "It pains me to think with all your education you're going to be a waitress and it's all my fault."

"When we're back on our feet, I'll go back to school, but until then this may be our best option. We'll both be making sacrifices, but that's what families do for each other."

"I just don't think you working there is for the best."

"Well, one good thing," Jenny said. "If you work there, you can't gamble there."

"I didn't know that. Maybe I should get a job there, too."

"Very funny, Mom. Don't let me forget to call the insurance company tomorrow and get a referral for you."

Her mother went to her bedroom after dinner. Jenny knew she was depressed about Jack and would be for some time. Telling her about the casino job hadn't helped. Plus, she had told Jenny she had some early-morning appointments with potential sellers for the next morning.

While her mother was away tomorrow, Jenny planned to call their creditors and see if she could lower their payments along with making some inquiries about work. But for tonight, all she wanted was to forget her problems and think about nothing except what show to watch next. She didn't want to work at the casino either, but life wasn't always about what you wanted.

She had just washed the dinner dishes and settled down in front of the television when she heard a knock at the front door. She looked through the curtains of the front window to see Luke and Adam standing on the porch. Her stomach dropped. She knew it was only a matter of time before they sought her out. She just hadn't expected them tonight. Slowly, she walked to the door and opened it.

"About time," Luke said, not hiding his anger.

"What do you want?"

"Let's take a walk," he said, glaring at her.

"Just say what you came to say."

"Where's your mother?"

"She's in bed. "

"Good. But I still think we should take this outside. Let's go."

"You're under the misconception that you can order me around. Just because we were together last night doesn't give you that right. Nothing gives you that right. So, like I said, say what you came to say."

"Have it your way," he said, pushing past her. Adam followed him inside. "Hello, Jenny."

"Hello, Adam."

"So you did it. You broke them up," Luke said, turning around as she closed the door.

"Now, Luke," Adam said calmly, "We don't know that for sure."

"I think we do."

"Maybe you should listen to your brother," she said, her back still to the both of them.

She felt what she assumed was Luke's hand on her arm. She tried to shrug it off but found his viselike grip to be firm. He turned her around. Her eyes met his in defiance. She wasn't going to let him push her around. He knew nothing, and that was the way it was going to stay. She remained silent.

"Why did you do it? What possessed you to want to ruin their happiness? Are you really that selfish?"

"Take your hand off my arm," she warned.

Luke dropped his hand as if he had been burned. However, he didn't move. His eyes dared her to look away.

"My mother broke up with your father because it was what she knew she had to do. It's been a long time coming. Trust me, I had nothing to do with it," she lied.

"Our dad is beside himself, Jenny," Adam said, standing next to Luke. "I haven't seen him this upset since…" He faltered. "Let's just say in a long time. He doesn't understand. Your mother just said she couldn't see him anymore. No explanation."

"I'm sorry about your dad." That was the truth.

"Are you really?" Luke's sarcasm was not lost on her.

"Yes, I am. I like your dad. I always have."

"None of this makes sense except that this is what you wanted, and Adam and I both know your mother would do anything for you. You mean the world to her. She obviously puts you ahead of her own happiness." Luke turned and walked into the living room, his shoulders slumped.

Adam continued to look at her, his eyes sad. "Don't you want your mother to be happy?"

"Of course I do. But I know you think they belong together. My mother has said things that make me believe otherwise."

"What things?" Luke shot back, walking back to where she and Adam were standing.

"Things that are her business and not for me to talk about with you or anyone. My mother's a grown woman, and she knows what she needs and unfortunately for your father, he's not what she needs."

"Tell us why you think he's not what she needs," Adam said, his voice suddenly hard and unyielding. "We need to know. My father needs to know."

"I can't. Trust me when I tell you it really is for the best."

"Best for them or best for you?" Luke asked harshly, his jaw rigid.

"You should both go now." Jenny felt like she was being attacked, and she didn't like it.

"And I think otherwise," Luke said. "In fact, I think it's your mother I should be speaking to."

"Oh, so you're going to speak with my mother about this? And then what, report back to your father that you think you can handle his love life better than he can?"

"God, you can be a bitch."

"You and your brother make me think my mother was more than justified in cutting your father loose. She doesn't need a man who sends his sons to fight his battles."

"Son of a bitch," Luke choked out, his face turning a deep shade of red. "Do you really hate the thought of your mother being with another man so badly you'd stoop so low as to try and degrade my father? He doesn't even know we're here."

Jenny immediately felt shame wash over her. However, this was no time to back down. She had to continue the charade or all would be lost, and her mother might never get better. "Our fighting won't change anything. Go home and stop putting your nose in where it doesn't belong."

Luke took a step toward her. Jenny backed away. She knew Luke was close to his breaking point. His anger was palpable. For the first time, she felt afraid.

"Luke," Adam said in warning, his hand on his brother's arm. "She's right. We should go. This isn't getting us anywhere."

"This isn't over," Luke said, turning to his brother. "I'm not going to let her destroy what Dad and Marlene have."

His eyes returned to Jenny. "You aren't going to get away with this. I promise you that." Luke turned sharply on his heels and stormed out the front door.

Adam took a deep breath before he spoke. "You have to know this is killing him and me. This isn't just about our parents. It's about us. You, me, Luke, and Justin. What happened between us wasn't some random thing, just like what's between our parents isn't either. He's not going to let you or your mother go, and neither am I. So be prepared, Jenny. We don't like to lose, and when the stakes are this high, we seldom ever do."

"I'm sorry your dad's hurt. It's not what I wanted." She felt terrible about everything, and she understood their anger and concern, however, they had to let this go for her mother's sake, and she couldn't allow them to intimidate her into telling them about her mother's problem and the real reason for the breakup.

"I think you're hiding something. You better come clean with us, Jenny, or you're not going to like the results."

Jenny felt the blood drain from her face. Although his voice was calm, it was like a knife slicing through her. She had no doubt that Adam would be as relentless as Luke in his search for the truth. However, recalling Luke's words, *when the stakes were this high*, she knew she would do whatever she had to keep her mother's secret even if it meant that the three men that had made her feel things she hadn't thought possible hated her.

"Don't threaten me, Adam. It doesn't become you."

"And lying doesn't become you. I thought you were better than that. But it looks like I was wrong about you. You're a destructive force in your mother's life and now my father's, to say nothing of your own. Hurting the people you love doesn't become you."

"You better leave. Your brother's waiting for you."

Adam turned and walked out the door. She shut it. Her whole body was trembling. She had never had a confrontation like that with anyone.

"What was all the yelling about?"

Jenny looked up to see her mother standing at the top of the stairs. How much, she wondered, had she heard?

Chapter Twelve

What a difference a few weeks can make. Jenny shut the door to her dad's old truck. Her mother was in therapy, and she was working. And despite Luke's and Adam's threats, she hadn't seen them since that night at her house. Maybe she and her mother could get through this.

Jenny walked quickly to the employee entrance of the Redwood Casino and slid her ID badge through the card reader and waited for the door to unlock. Once inside, she walked up the escalator to the casino offices and the staff locker room.

She had three costumes, and she kept all three at work. She had no desire to wear them back and forth to work like some of the girls, and besides that, the casino had them dry-cleaned free of charge, so there was no need to bring them home. But more than that, all her mother needed was to be reminded of where she worked. It was enough that she had taken the job against her mother's wishes.

"No, Jenny," her mother had all but yelled when she finally had found the nerve to tell her that Anne had helped her get the job. "You can't work there. You'll be nothing but a sex object encouraging people to drink too much and gamble even more. It's not right."

"It may not be right in your mind, but it's going to help us pay the bills. I'm lucky I got it. There are plenty of people out there looking for work, and this job pays well. We need it."

"There has to be something else. You just have to look harder."

"I told you before there isn't anything around here that has the earning potential of working at the casino. I'm sorry, but I have to do this."

When her mother shook her head and silently walked away, Jenny knew she had won, but it wasn't the kind of victory she enjoyed. Her mother's shoulders were slumped and she knew what was going through her mind. She was blaming herself. However, what choice did she have when they were so desperate for money?

Jenny hurried to the locker room and slipped into the gold-and-black corset that lifted her large breasts upward and outward. It would have been nice if it were a little less revealing, but there were no other options if she wanted to keep her job.

Once she had clocked in, she went to the manager's office to get her assignment. Michael, the assistant manager, was waiting for her with a smile on his face.

"Hey there, Jenny. As always, it's good to see you."

"Thanks."

"I'm putting you on the poker tables, one through ten. That should keep you busy. We have a good crowd tonight."

"Good. I like the poker tables. The tips are usually very good."

"Samantha will be waiting for you. She's anxious to get home. She did a double today."

"Wow. Did someone call out sick?"

"Yeah, your friend, Anne. She called out three times this week. I'm beginning to wish I hadn't hired her, but then again, she did recommend you."

"I don't think she'd call out unless she had to."

"Well, if she continues, I will have to let her go. It's not fair to the other girls."

"I'm sure she has a good excuse," Jenny said, not wishing to continue the conversation that made her uncomfortable. "I better relieve Samantha. See you later."

"Definitely," he said, his eyes looking her up and down.

She turned quickly and walked out of his office. Michael had an eye for the ladies, but he was harmless. She had been told by a couple of the other girls that he had a wife he adored along with three kids.

She hoped they were right. The last thing she needed or wanted was anything to complicate or threaten her job. Her mother might not approve, but it was turning out to be exactly what they needed to stay ahead of the creditors and keep the house.

"Jenny, you're here a little early, and am I glad," Samantha said, walking up to her with a tray full of drinks. "I'll deliver these and be right back."

Jenny watched Samantha walk away with a deliberate sway to her hips. She was almost six feet tall and was all curves. The men at the tables couldn't take their eyes off her, for all the good it would do them. She was engaged to two professional football players who she said didn't mind that she worked serving drinks to men who ogled her. They were confident in her and knew she loved the work. Jenny could understand they trusted her, but why Samantha liked to serve drinks to men who undressed her with their eyes was something she would never be able to figure out. She knew as soon as she could, she would give her notice, but that, unfortunately, wouldn't be for some time.

When Samantha returned, she gave Jenny a rundown on the tables and then took off. The only table that had given her any problems was filled with old men who looked like they were ready for the nursing home. She supposed they thought age gave them certain rights. She'd be nice to them but not overly friendly. Luckily, they behaved themselves and were generous with the tips.

By the end of her shift, her feet hurt. She hated the spiked heels she had to wear, and would have given anything to be able to wear sneakers or even a pair of low-heeled shoes. She was delivering her last tray of drinks when she looked over at the table next to her. She felt as if the wind had been knocked out of her. Luke Rowan and his cousin Justin were staring her, and if looks could kill, she would have dropped to the floor from a heart attack. Holding on to her tray securely, she took a deep a breath and delivered her drinks without spilling a drop.

When she was done, she didn't look back and walked directly to the bar where she hoped her replacement would be waiting for her. She breathed a sigh of relief when she saw Roseanne talking with the bartender.

"How's business tonight?" the pretty blonde asked her.

"It's good, Roseanne, and no one looks like they're leaving. You should have a good morning."

"That's why I'm here," she said with a smile.

They talked for a few minutes about the tables. It was standard practice to make sure your replacement knew what to expect. She was happy there wasn't much to talk about. All she could think about was getting off the casino floor and away from Luke and Justin. The last time she had seen Luke, he had been anything but pleasant, and she wasn't looking forward to another yelling session. She was too tired to cope with it or the onset of one of her migraines that she knew had to be stress related. She still hadn't been to a doctor.

Changing her clothes as fast as she could, she practically ran out of the casino and to her truck. She had just unlocked the door when she heard footsteps behind her.

"You're in a big hurry."

Luke's voice caused her back to stiffen. "I am," she said, opening the truck door.

"I forgot your mother had kept your father's truck."

"No reason why you would remember," she said, turning to face him. "What do you want? I'm too tired to fight with you again."

"I don't want to fight with you either. Just thought Justin and I would say hello, and since you didn't stick around, we decided to come looking for you."

"Cut the crap, Luke. You didn't find me to just say hello."

"Would you believe me if I said I missed you, that we all missed you?"

"Right, I don't have time for this. Have to go."

"Come back to Justin's with us. Adam's there."

Jenny knew she should just get in the truck and drive off, but something in Luke's tone of voice stopped her. He had a lot of nerve, but her body was responding to his demand even if her brain was telling her it was nothing but a ploy to get information about their parents' breakup. She had missed them…a lot. She hadn't wanted to admit it, but not a day or especially a night went by that she didn't think about what it was like to be in their bed. She groaned silently, wishing he weren't standing so close to her.

"That's not a good idea," she said, hoping he would simply let her go and not say anything else. She needed to get away from him and Justin. Justin's eyes were all but devouring her. She felt her resolve weakening. She was tired and that made her vulnerable.

Maybe they heard the weakness in her voice, because Justin suddenly pushed forward and grabbed her hand. "We won't do anything you don't want us to. It's just that you're all we can think about. We won't talk about your mom, promise. Come with us, Jenny."

"I can't."

"Yes, you can," Luke said, drawing her to him. "Yes, you can."

"I thought you hated me," she said breathlessly.

"Hate's a mighty strong word. Believe me when I say, I don't hate you. I want you, we all do. Tell me you don't think about that night."

Jenny lowered her eyes. She was losing the battle between her body and her brain. She could feel her resolve weakening. Why were they doing this to her? Maybe to prove that they could. If she went with them, she would end up doing whatever they wanted. Did they think she would tell them what they wanted to know? She couldn't change that, no matter how much her body wanted to have them inside her.

"No." She turned and got in the truck, slamming the door behind her. She put the key in the ignition but nothing happened. She tried it again. Nothing but clicking. Not now, she prayed as she tried to start the truck again. Luke and Justin were standing outside her window. She rolled it down.

"Won't start? Want me to try it?"

She nodded at Justin and got back out of the truck.

He got in and Luke went to the hood of the truck and opened it. He wiggled a few wires, and Justin tried it again. Nothing. After a few more attempts, Luke shut the hood of the truck and walked over to her.

"Dead as a doornail I'm afraid. Looks like us being here turned out to be a good thing after all."

Justin shut the truck door behind him. "Can we give you a ride?" He smiled.

"I guess the answer to that question would be yes. I'll need a ride after all. This is the first time the truck has given me any trouble."

"We're parked on the other side of the casino," Justin said.

Silently, they walked back into the casino and to the exit for the customer parking lot. Luke clicked the remote, and the lights on his Land Rover blinked a few times. He opened the door for her and she slid into front passenger seat. Justin crawled into the back as Luke slid into the driver's seat and started the car.

"Put on your seat belt, Jenny," he said, his eyes watching her as she did as he instructed.

"That's a good girl. We'll come back for your truck tomorrow."

"It will probably have to be towed," she said with a sigh. *How much is this going to cost?* She would have to have it repaired. She needed it.

"I have a friend that might be able to take a look at it. We'll see."

"Luckily, I don't work tomorrow."

"Good," Justin said from the backseat. "Everyone should have Sunday off. The casino should be closed at least one day."

"It's open twenty-four-seven, it never closes," Jenny said. "However, I do agree with you."

"Did you just say you agree with Justin? Did I hear you right?"

"I'm not that disagreeable, am I?"

Luke kept his eyes on the road as he pulled out of the parking lot onto the highway. When he glanced her way, his eyes lingered on her face before they lowered to her breasts. She could feel the heat from his stare before he turned his attention back to his driving. "We'll be home before you know it," he said almost as if he were talking to himself.

She was going to say and *you're taking me straight to my home*, but she knew that wasn't going to happen. Her panties were wet and her nipples were hard. She hated herself for wanting them so badly. They were going to take her to Justin's, and she wasn't going to stop them because, God help her, that's what she wanted.

Chapter Thirteen

Adam opened the door. Jenny smiled shyly, feeling slightly intimidated by the man standing in front of her. His lips were set in a firm line. He didn't look pleased.

"I guess your mother's confession gave you a change of heart?"

"My mother's confession." She repeated what Adam had just said. "What are you talking about?"

"Damn it, Adam." Luke shook his head with a sigh, brushing past Jenny. "We were going to get to that."

Jenny looked from one man to the other with dread. "What did my mother tell you?"

"Your mother told my father about her gambling problem," Adam said, using the voice she imagined he did with patients who were being told bad news. "Did you really think we wouldn't find out?"

"I'm sorry, Jenny," Justin said from behind her. "Sorry for everything that's happened to you, but I'm also sorry that you felt you couldn't confide in us yourself."

"When did you find out?"

"Dad and Marlene told us tonight," Luke said.

"And you couldn't wait to see me and rub my nose in our problems that I'm sure your father will make go away with a wave of his checkbook? My mother will be indebted to him for life."

"She hates the fact that you work there," Justin said, gently pushing her body through the open doorway before he closed the door behind them. "She told us you'd be there and what time you got off."

"And my truck didn't just not start by itself, did it? What did you do?" She already knew the answer.

"I'll go back tomorrow and reattach the sparkplugs," Luke said without any shame in his voice. "We needed to talk to you about your mother and my father. I had a feeling you'd get your back up when you knew your mother had finally done the right thing and told my dad the truth. Taking away your ride was all I could think of to get you back here with us."

"Smart," Adam said, looking at his brother and then Justin. "And a bit devious, but it did work."

"You're right, I would have never come with you," Jenny said, feeling a wave of anger overcoming her. "I can't believe she went to your father and told him. I told her we could dig ourselves out of the mess she created without anyone's help. I thought she never wanted your father to know, for anyone to know for that matter."

Jenny felt Justin's hand on her elbow and allowed him to guide her into the living room where she sat on the sofa. This was all too much. She never expected her mother to turn on her. But she had, and it was all too clear to her that Jack Rowan meant a lot more to her mother than her own daughter.

"Here, take a drink of this," Adam said, handing her a glass of wine. "You look like you could use a drink."

She took it. She needed a lot more than a glass of wine. She suddenly felt reckless. "And did she also tell your father that she's been in love him with since they were in high school? That my father was her consolation prize?"

"What are you talking about?" Luke asked, his voice low.

"That's what I thought," she said with a smirk. "Of course she didn't."

"I knew they went to high school together, but Dad never mentioned they had dated." Adam was looking at her like she had two heads.

"Well they did until he went away to school, and she waited for him. But he brought your mother home with him and that was the end of that."

"That doesn't mean she was still in love with him," Adam said calmly. "I'm sure it was totally over before Dad married Mom."

"Over for your father, maybe, but not my mom. She's been waiting years for a chance to get back with him. How convenient that my father and your mother died."

"Jenny!" Luke said, his voice harsh. "That's a horrible thing to say and untrue. What you're implying is sick."

Adam just stared at her before he said, "Your mother was devastated when your father died. You can't fake that kind of grief."

"I'm not saying she didn't care for him, but she wasn't in love with him. If she was, she wouldn't have gone to your father so easily, and she'd have never told him about what she did just to try and keep him with her, knowing she was humiliating her family."

"Jenny," Justin spoke softly. "I think you have this all wrong. I know my uncle and he loved my aunt very much, and from the little I know of your mother, she would never coldly calculate what you're accusing her of."

"She had guilt. That I believe. That's why she gambled. To escape what she had done and was doing. She knew being with your uncle was wrong. That she was disrespecting my father's memory. But obviously," she said, taking a gulp of the wine, "she couldn't or wouldn't stop herself from doing exactly what she had denied herself all those years. Or, at least, I think she denied herself. Who knows, maybe they had an ongoing illicit affair for all I know."

"They didn't," Luke said, taking her arm and turning her towards him. "My father was never disloyal to my mother. I can tell you that for sure."

"Can you? You don't know. You just don't want to believe it."

"Luke's right. They never did. And if you ever breathe a word of that to anyone, so help me God," Adam said, his face red with anger.

"You'll do what? Make me regret it?" Jenny knew she should stop, but the recklessness she had felt had turned to anger and vengeance. She had loved her father, and the more she thought about her mother's confession, the angrier she became. She had not only taken her father's trust and thrown it away, but she had taken hers and done the same.

"My God, you're a spoiled brat," Luke all but spat out. "You'll do anything to try and keep them apart even if it means spouting lies on top of lies." Luke's face had turned even more red than Adam's.

"I bet you'd like to punish me, wouldn't you?" Her voice had gone silky and low.

"If you mean turn you over my knee and give you the spanking you never got as a child, then the answer is yes."

She suddenly felt the anger drain from her to be replaced with something else, something much different. She couldn't take her eyes off Adam's.

"Then do it," she breathed, her voice trembling, but not with fear.

When none of them spoke, she continued, knowing she was on dangerous ground but not caring. Her mother wasn't going to deny herself, so why should she?

"I respond well to a firm hand." She picked herself up off the sofa and put what was left of her wine down on an end table. She walked to the center of the room. They watched her, still not uttering even a syllable.

Slowly she let her jacket fall to the ground and kicked it with her foot. She began to unbutton her shirt while swaying her hips. She let it drop to the floor. What was she doing? She should stop, but she didn't want to. She wanted them to take her like they had before. Maybe she was more like her mother than she wanted to believe. After Jack Rowan paid off their debt, she and her mother would never be free of the Rowan men, so why fight it? When she undid her pants and began to pull them down, it was Justin that broke the silence.

"Jenny, don't do this," he said, his voice husky. "Put your clothes back on and I'll take you home."

"Do what he says," Luke said.

"They're right," Adam said softly. "I want you, but not like this. You're angry and hurt, and being with us isn't going to be your punishment."

"No, it's not," she agreed. "Fucking the three of you is far from punishment. I've wanted you ever since that night you took me in every way imaginable. I want you to fuck me. I need you to fuck me like you did. Don't tell me you don't want me." She couldn't believe she was talking like this, but she wasn't lying. She wanted them desperately, and she was going to have her way whether they thought it was wrong or not. She wanted to forget everything except the way they felt inside her.

"Jenny," Adam said, his voice thick, "we should take you home."

"No, you shouldn't. Not now." She finished taking her jeans off and kicked them over to the side as she had her jacket and shirt. She bent down and untied her sneakers and took them off along with her socks. Standing in just bra and panties, she unhooked her bra and let her breasts spill free. She wanted them to see how swollen they were with her need. Her hard nipples ached for their touch. Hooking her thumbs in her panties, she slid them down her body until they were around her ankles. She lifted her foot and pushed them away.

Slipping onto her knees, she ran her hands over her breasts and touched her pussy. She heard them groan. They were going to take her or they would have already been helping her put her clothes back on. She had them just where she wanted them.

"Spank me, Luke. I need to be spanked," she said, her voice full and husky.

"Come here," Luke said gruffly.

She crawled to him. He drew her upward and over his knee. She waited patiently for him to begin. Her pussy was so wet. Her juices were dripping down her thighs. She moaned softly in anticipation. The first smack against her tender cheeks made her jump. The second even more so. Three more followed in succession, each more forceful than the last. She bit her lip, knowing she wanted more.

"Get up, Jenny."

Reluctantly, she lifted herself only to see that Adam and Justin were standing with her clothes in their hands.

"Now get dressed. You're going home."

"What?"

"You heard me. Get dressed. I want you. We all do. But when we take you next, it will be with love and not to satisfy your need to put us in our place."

"But I thought," she said, feeling suddenly ashamed, "I thought you wanted me like this."

"We do," Adam said, handing her panties and bra. "Now put these back on and quickly or I'll do it for you."

She grabbed her panties first and slipped them on. Her bra was next. Justin handed her socks, pants, and her shirt. She didn't want to cry, but the humiliation and revelations of the night flooded her consciousness. Somehow she managed to pull on her sneakers, but it was Justin who tied them for her.

"It's okay, Jenny," he said, putting both hands on her cheeks to wipe away her tears after he was through tying her shoes. "It's all going to be okay. You'll see. Now, stop the tears. Your mother's waiting up for you."

"You were never going to take me to your bed tonight," she said, realizing now their intentions had been anything but sexual.

"We wanted to talk to you before you saw your mother," Luke said. "I thought we needed to prepare you so she wouldn't have to explain everything. She's extremely emotional. Telling my father and then us about her problem took a lot out of her. She needs you, Jenny, and she needs you to be supportive.

"She doesn't need your condemnation. She needs your understanding," he continued. "If you truly want her to get well, you have to put all that stuff you told us behind you. She loves you so much. In the state she's in, you could destroy her with your words."

"I love my mother," she choked out. "I just wish things hadn't gotten so out of control. I don't know what to say to her now. Her going back with your father makes me wonder if she ever loved my father."

"I can't speak for your mother," Luke said softly, "but answer me this, was she a good wife and mother?"

Jenny nodded. "Yes. That's what's so hard. She was."

"Did your father love her?"

She nodded again. "Yes, I know he did. He adored her. I saw the love in his eyes."

"Then that's your answer. Nothing else matters. Your father loved her and would want her to be happy. I know she loved him, too. But she and my father have a second chance to love and be loved again. Don't deny them that, Jenny. It would be cruel."

Luke was right. She had been behaving like a spoiled brat. Making her mother break up with the man she loved had been her own way of punishing her for losing the money and for loving another man.

"I should have encouraged her to tell the truth to him instead of hiding it, but she said she didn't want anyone to know, and I blamed him, too."

"She said a lot of things. She was desperate and ashamed. But that's over now. My father's going to help her, and we're going to help you." Adam's eyes were kind.

She looked around and saw that all three men were looking at her with compassion and, it seemed, love. Could they really love her? Especially after the way she had acted. What did she really know about love? Nothing. That was her answer.

"Now come here," Justin said, holding out his arms.

She melted into them and buried her face in his chest. Luke and Adam followed, their arms wrapping themselves around her. "Why are you being so nice to me?"

"I think it's pretty obvious," Justin said, "but that's a conversation for another day. Right now, we need to get you home to your mother."

Chapter Fourteen

The days and weeks that followed her mother's confession went by in a whirlwind. Jenny was amazed at how easily Jack had taken control of her mother's life and how easily she had let him. Her mother was in counseling, and she and Jack were also seeing a therapist together. He had insisted that he be a part of her recovery. Jenny knew he wanted her to see someone, too. However, she wasn't sure exactly why, but the idea of pouring out her emotions to a complete stranger made her feel ill. Whenever she seriously contemplated doing what they both wanted, she felt one of those visual migraines coming on. It was a definite sign, she told herself, that therapy wasn't for her.

Luke, Adam, and Justin all agreed with Jack and her mother, but they had let the subject of her seeing a therapist drop when she had threatened to never see any of them again. It was an idle threat, but they seemed to take her seriously. Although they continued to be more than supportive of both her and her mother, they had made no move to rekindle any romantic feelings between the four of them. If anything, they seemed to be avoiding any physical contact with her. It was unnerving. She felt like her mind and body were being stretched to their breaking point. She wanted them, but she couldn't humble herself like that again.

The last time they were together, she had stripped for them, received a spanking, and then was taken home without the fulfillment she had needed so badly. She had felt totally humiliated, yet her desire for them continued to intensify with each day she was in their company but not their bed. They were driving her crazy. She needed to forget about them in that way. When she eventually went back to school, it would be a lot easier. However, taking money from Jack Rowan would never sit well with her.

Today she was supposed to meet with April Mathews about the summer festival. Luke had volunteered her to help with the decorating and whatever else needed to be done. She had wanted to say no only because he had just assumed she would do it. However, it was for a good cause, and now that she wasn't working at the casino, she needed something to do, even if it meant she would have to suffer April's company.

Hopping into her truck, she forced herself to drive to April's house. There were a number of cars in the driveway of the sprawling farm house. It had pretty light-blue shutters and an assortment of flowers decorating the window boxes. To her surprise, she felt herself drawn to the friendliness the house seemed to radiate.

April came out of the front door and stood on the front steps. She waved to Jenny. "Hey, Jenny. We're just about ready to begin. I'm glad you could make it."

"Sorry. I was running a little late. I hope I didn't hold you up."

"Come on in and meet everyone."

Jenny followed April through to the back of the house where there was a huge kitchen. It was filled with around ten women who all stopped talking when she entered the room.

"Okay, ladies, for those of you who haven't met or haven't seen Jenny in years, this is Jenny Clayton. Her mother is Marlene Clayton, who if you own a house, probably sold it to you. She's volunteered to help, and I for one am very happy to have here with us."

Jenny couldn't have been more surprised at April's introduction. What, she wondered, had changed since the last time she saw her. It didn't take long for her to find out.

They had broken down into three committees. Jenny was working with April and a woman called Sandy on the sports and entertainment. It was the foundation of the festival. There were a variety of races, softball games, and this year they were hoping to have a talent competition. April was writing everything down when her cell phone rang. She glanced at it and then smiled widely.

"Excuse me. I have to take this."

Sandy followed April with her eyes, a big smile on her own face. "I would imagine that's one of the Landers brothers. She's been on cloud nine ever since they all got back together. I'm so happy for her."

"Me, too," Jenny said, wondering why she hadn't known about this. She would have thought Luke or Adam would have mentioned it.

"I wasn't sure they would, you know, get back together. April was devastated when she thought they had been untrue to her with the town slut, Jillian, but things aren't always the way they seem, and luckily she was able to see through it."

"Do you mean Jillian Palmer?"

"Yes, do you know her?" Sandy asked, her eyes narrowing.

"She was in one of my classes in high school. We worked on a few projects together. She always seemed nice."

"Yeah, she was nice all right, especially to the boys."

Thinking it was best to steer the conversation away from Jillian Palmer, Jenny said, "Well, I'm glad that April is back with the Landers brothers. That's all that's important."

Before Sandy could respond, April returned, still smiling. "Okay, any more ideas on the talent contest?"

By the time the meeting was over, Jenny had ideas for the posters that she said she would create and post all over town. Sandy was going to take care of the staging and the tent. April said she was going make an announcement at church and also put it in the church bulletin as well as speak to various businesses and the local dance studio.

When Jenny offered to talk to her old boss at the casino about some props and things to help Sandy, April frowned.

"I didn't think you worked there anymore?"

"Who told you that?"

"I don't know."

"Well, I don't. But I left on good terms, and there's nothing wrong with asking them for help, is there?"

"No. And there's no reason to be defensive. Sorry I brought it up." April turned to follow Sandy, who had already walked away toward the front of the house.

"I know my mother's going to marry Jack Rowan, but that doesn't mean his sons or his nephew tell me what to do. I decided to quit on my own."

"Of course they don't," April said, stopping to turn around. "Why are you so upset?"

"I'm not."

"You could have fooled me. Seems like you got a real bug up your butt when it comes to the casino, or is it the Rowans?"

Jenny looked down at her hands that she used to smooth down her skirt. April was a lot more perceptive than she had given her credit for, but it really was none of her business.

"I know. I'm the last person you want to discuss the Rowan men and their cousin Justin with, but if you want to, I'd be glad to listen. Now that I'm back with my men, I guess I want everyone else to be happy, too."

"Did any of them talk to you about me? I mean, not that I care, but it's good to know what people are saying about you."

"Luke's mentioned you a few times. So did Adam and Justin. You're on their mind a lot. I'd say they're on your mind a lot, too."

"My mother's in love with Jack Rowan, and she's going to be a part of their family. I'm just an interloper as far as they are concerned."

"An interloper. I don't think so."

"Whatever," Jenny said, wishing the conversation was over.

"Come with me," April said.

"Where?"

"I want to show you something. Just let me say good-bye to everyone, and I'll be right back."

Jenny was confused, but nodded as April smiled and walked away. Within a few minutes she was back with a set of car keys in her hand. "Let's take a drive."

They had been driving for almost fifteen minutes when April turned off onto a dirt road. Jenny couldn't imagine what it was she wanted to show her. "We're a little far out aren't we?"

"Yes. But once you see it, you'll understand."

They drove into a clearing that looked out onto a lake. It was beautiful. April got out of the car and motioned for Jenny to follow her. This, Jenny thought, was really getting weird. Where on earth was Jenny taking her?

They hadn't walked for long when Jenny saw a house through the trees. She gasped at the sheer size of the house that was still under construction. It was magnificent. Jenny thought it must qualify as a mansion regardless of the rustic exterior. "Is this yours?"

"No, although maybe someday I'll have a place like this. It's Jack Rowan's wedding present for your mother."

"What?"

"Justin's company has been building it. They showed it to me."

"You must spend a lot of time with the three of them."

"We're all just friends now. I've got my men. I'm showing you this because, even though you act like you hate them, I know better. And I wanted you see how much Jack Rowan adores and loves your mother. He'd do anything to make her happy."

"This house doesn't mean love. It just means he has a lot of money and he can buy what he wants, including my mother."

"That's so not true. Why would you say that?"

"It doesn't matter what I think. My mom's going to love it."

"Are you jealous?" April asked hesitantly, then said, "I shouldn't have said that. I'm sorry. It's just I've never heard Luke speak of anyone the way he does you, and you seem to have so much anger inside of you. It doesn't make sense."

Jenny turned away from April, lowering her yes, her voice barely audible, "What does he say about me?"

"Oh, Jenny, you're in love with him, I knew it!"

"April, please, stop. They're going to be my brothers, and their cousin will be my cousin, too. They're not mine to love."

"You love all three of them." April gasped, her face breaking into a wide grin. "This is wonderful."

"Are you kidding? You can't be serious. I'm not in love with them, and there's nothing wonderful about it."

"You can tell me, Jenny."

Maybe it was the sincerity in April's voice or maybe she was just tired of pretending. Whatever it was, she couldn't believe she was about to cry and spill her guts to the one person, April Mathews, she had never really even liked and would have never thought to bring into her confidence. But here she was with April and the tears were already flowing.

"I do love them," she choked. "But they"—she wiped her eyes— "don't feel that way about me. They hate me for trying to break up my mother and Jack. They can't forgive me, even though they have to know I did it for what I thought were the right reasons."

"Have you tried to sit down and talk to them about how you feel?"

"Of course not. They've been pretty clear about how they feel about me. The last time I tried to give myself to them, they rejected me."

"You need to tell them, Jenny. They're men, and men don't just get things like we do. They have to be told or at least they have to be shown and sometimes more than once. If you're not willing to go to them, at least one more time, you may regret it forever. Believe me, I know."

"It obviously worked for you," Jenny said, trying to smile. "You got your men back or they got you back."

"It was mutual. We needed to talk, but mostly I needed to listen."

"I think it's too late for me. I just can't put myself out there again."

"If you love them as much as I think you do, you will. You have to. Don't let your pride keep you from what you want, from you what you need."

Jenny gazed at the house in front of her. It was beautiful and her mother would love it. And, she knew her mother really did love Jack Rowan. He would make her happy. Did the past really matter anymore? Maybe, if she could think more about the future, she could find the strength to try and talk to Luke, Adam, and Justin one more time.

Chapter Fifteen

Jenny had been trying to find the right moment to confront the men she had finally admitted she loved and wanted in life as her husbands and not as just family. However, she was still unsure of how she would be received, and that was making her incredibly shy around them whenever she was in their company. Even her mother had asked if they had said or done something to offend her. She was a mass of nerves, and she wasn't sure she would ever feel comfortable enough with them to declare herself. It was all so complicated.

Her mother and Jack had gone away for the weekend to a concert in Chicago. Jenny hadn't even spoken with the boys about what they were doing. She had just assumed they were busy, too. She wanted to call one of them, but each time she thought about it, she felt at a loss for words. She also felt the twinges of a migraine and that, she told herself, was reason enough to postpone calling them.

So when the telephone rang and it was Luke, she felt her heart leap into her throat.

"Luke?"

"Hi, Jenny. How are you?"

"Fine."

"Are you busy?"

"No."

"We're making dinner, Justin, Adam, and I. We thought you might like to join us since your mom is away with my dad."

"Yes. That sounds really nice."

"Good."

She hung up the phone and took a deep breath. Luke had sounded awkward, almost shy. Did he think she was going to say no? Picking herself up from the sofa, she ran up the steps to her bedroom. She wanted to look especially nice tonight. She wanted to make them want her. Was she prepared to do whatever she needed to? She could only hope.

Adam opened the door and ushered her inside. He was dressed in a light-blue tailored shirt and a pair of gray pants that fit him to perfection. Both Luke and Justin came into the living room to greet her. They looked delicious, too. She subconsciously licked her lips, her eyes devouring the three men. She felt the warmth between her legs increase. She needed to step back and take control of her emotions that threatened to make a fool of her.

"Hello," she said softly.

"My, don't you look pretty," Luke said, his eyes looking her up and down.

"Yes," Justin and Adam said in unison.

"Thank you. And thank you for inviting me for dinner. That was nice of you."

"We weren't sure you would come," Justin said, his eyes resting on her exposed skin and cleavage that the little black dress she wore encouraged.

"I've been wanting to have some time alone with the three of you," she began.

"Really," Luke said, "and why is that?"

"We can talk after dinner," she said, no longer feeling quite so confident.

"Of course, we can," Adam said, coming to her rescue. "And it's ready. Take my arm and I'll take you into the dining room."

"What does Astrid have for us tonight?" Jenny smiled, looking up into Adam's eyes.

"Actually," he said. "We made dinner. Astrid is visiting with her granddaughter for the next few weeks and we gave the staff off. We're alone here tonight."

"Oh," Jenny said, surprised. "I'm sure it will be great."

"We'll see. I hope you like spaghetti. It's one of the few things we know how to make that we'd serve to company."

"I'm not company. I'm family or least I will be soon."

"I'd like to think you're a lot more than family," Adam said, holding out her chair.

She felt a shiver of anticipation shoot through her body. She wanted to think that, too. She just hoped he meant it.

The meal was good, not great. The meatballs were a little tough and the sauce could have used more garlic. However, it could have all tasted like hay for all Jenny cared. What she hungered for was the company of these three men and more. It was the more that kept her balancing herself on the end of her chair throughout the meal. She could hardly sit still with all the feelings that were out of control and coursing through her body.

They were polite and attentive to her every need. She thought if they asked her one more question about the meal she was going to jump out of her skin. All she wanted was to take off her clothes and offer herself to them. Instead, she excused herself to go to the bathroom. They all stood as she walked out of the room.

When she returned, the table had already been cleared. There was coffee and what looked like a four dessert cups filled with strawberry parfait. She smiled.

"Doesn't this look good."

She sat down and scooped out a spoonful of the dessert. It was delicious. "Oh my, this is fantastic."

"April made them for us," Luke said. "She promised they would be great."

"April made the dessert? She knew I was coming for dinner?"

"I hope you don't mind that we told her," Adam said. "It was her idea."

"To make the dessert or my coming over for dinner?"

"Both," Luke said.

"She told us that it would be the perfect time to talk to you, and from what you said when you walked in tonight, you wanted to talk to us, too. I think we all have to agree, it's been entirely too awkward between us."

"So, I have April to thank for you wanting to see me." Jenny felt deflated, and she couldn't keep the disappointment out of her voice.

"She's not the reason we wanted you to come to dinner. She just gave us the nudge we needed even though we were sure you wouldn't want to be alone with us. She thought we should at least ask."

"I'm glad she did," Jenny conceded. "We needed to do this. The last time we were alone, it didn't end well. At least I didn't think it did."

"We did what we thought was for the best, or at least what we thought you needed," Justin began.

"Maybe we were wrong," Luke said. "Maybe I was wrong. It seems I made you hate us."

"Hate you? I don't hate you."

"No? Then why does it seem like you cringe whenever you're in the same room with us? Don't tell me it's not true. Even our parents have noticed something was wrong." Adam's eyes looked deeply into hers. "Can we make it right again, Jenny? We want to, so badly."

Jenny knew it was now or never. She had to tell them the truth no matter what the outcome. Even if they didn't want her, at least they could start fresh without any preconceived notions of what their feelings were or were not.

"I don't hate you," she said, lowering her voice, "you see, I'm love with you and…I wish I weren't, but I am, and knowing you don't feel the same way"—she looked down, unable to acknowledge what she could only imagine was sympathy in their eyes—"makes it hard for me to be around you."

"Jenny," Luke said, her name sounding like a caress, "Oh, Jenny, did you really say you loved us?"

She looked up, her heart turning over in her chest. Luke stood up, as did Adam and Justin. They couldn't get to her fast enough. She felt herself being lifted upward into all three of their arms. She couldn't tell where one began and the other ended. They were laughing and hugging her. She could only imagine that it meant one thing.

"We love you," Justin cried, his lips finding hers. "We love you so much."

Justin's kiss deepened, his tongue swirling with hers. She gasped when his lips left hers only to be replaced by Adam's and then Luke's. She was so engrossed in his kiss she hadn't realized that her dress had been unzipped and torn from her body. She was practically naked standing in Luke's arms. Her black lace panties and bra did little to hide her desire.

"Oh, my God, Jenny," Luke whispered into hair. "Do you know how tortured we've been, thinking you wanted nothing to do with us. Knowing we would be seeing you for the rest of our lives and that you wouldn't be ours?"

"I'm yours now and forever. I want all three of you more than I've ever wanted anything in my life."

She felt her panties and her bra being removed. She stepped away from Luke and kicked her panties away. Her bra disappeared. Their hands were caressing her. Adam held her breasts upward for both Justin and Luke to suck on her nipples. She groaned as her knees began to buckle.

Adam lowered her to the carpet next to the table. She spread her legs as Justin cupped her wet pussy. He fingered her as his lips descended to capture her mound in his mouth. Luke, now naked, stood above her, stroking his cock. He looked down into her eyes that she knew had to be a reflection of the love she saw in his.

She watched as Justin and Adam moved aside to remove their clothing. Luke lowered himself and with one stroke, he entered her. She all but screamed his name.

"I've been dreaming about this since the last time we were together. You have no idea how much I've wanted to make love to you, Jenny."

She felt his cum fill her pussy. "Please," was all she could say as she slipped into a world of emotions that ended in the climax she so needed.

He lifted himself from her. She saw him smile up at Justin and Adam. They were naked, and their cocks were hard and dripping pre-cum. She wanted them every bit as much as she had wanted Luke. Adam slid underneath her and slipped his cock inside her cum-filled pussy. Justin slid his cock between her ass cheeks. She moaned softly while Luke let her suck the remainder of his cum from his cock. She shivered with her need to come again.

Justin entered her swiftly, and she was ready for him. Adam began fucking her with firm, hard strokes. Luke removed his cock from her mouth and looked down her. His eyes were glazed with love and desire.

"You are everything to us, Jenny," he said, watching Justin and Adam give and take pleasure from her. "You're so beautiful, and watching you like this makes me happier than you could ever know."

She felt both Justin and Adam filling her with their cum. She closed her eyes and let the feelings of ecstasy wash over in wave after wave. Luke whispered words of love into her hair. She had never in all her life felt more loved or more content.

When she was completely saturated with their cum and their love, she opened her eyes. She kissed each man, not holding back, letting them feel the strength of her feeling for them. "I love you," she crooned over and over.

"Will you marry us?" Luke asked.

"Yes, I'll marry you," she said with tears in her eyes. She knew that no woman could or would ever be happier.

"Oh, and Jenny," Adam said, tearing himself away from her for a moment, "we have a surprise for you."

"What?" she asked and then laughed. "Will it always be like this with you three? One surprise after another?"

"What he wants to tell you," Justin said, looking over at Adam and then to Luke, "is that we're thinking of moving."

"Why would you want to move?"

"We want to be close to you while you're completing your PhD," Luke said before he smiled at her expectantly.

"Just when I thought I couldn't love you more," she said, the tears now flooding down her cheeks. "You would move for me?"

"Yes," Luke, Adam, and Justin said together.

"It's only until you complete your degree and then we can decide where we want to live permanently. As long as we're together, it doesn't matter where we live. We all have careers that give us flexibility," Adam said, holding her close.

"But your dad…he thinks you're taking over his practice."

"My dad understands what's important. And from what he tells us, he doesn't plan to retire anytime soon."

"Adam's right," Luke said. "Dad's like an old soldier. They don't retire, they just fade away. He'll be doctoring until the day he dies."

"And your mother," Justin added, "told me nothing would make her happier than knowing you were completing your degree."

"I don't know what to say other than I love you all so much."

Jenny was touched beyond words that they were willing to make a sacrifice of this magnitude by putting her happiness before their own. It had taken a while, but she finally understood what it meant to really love someone and to be loved in return. Adam was right. Nothing mattered as long as they were together, and her heart told her that would be forever.

THE END

ABOUT THE AUTHOR

Kalissa Alexander loves to write stories about love. She is a woman of diversified interests, from singing karaoke, to knitting, to creating her own crafts at the holidays. However, nothing brings her more pleasure than to write about desirable, loving women that regardless of life's obstacles always find true love with the men that can make their dreams come true. She believes that happy endings are what women not only want but need to believe in. On any given day or into the night, she can be found bringing her characters to life with an anxious smile as she finds the words to express their feelings in a story that makes them perfect for each other in an imperfect world. Life is full of possibilities; she enjoys bringing all of them to her readers.

For all titles by Kalissa Alexander, please visit
www.bookstrand.com/kalissa-alexander

Siren Publishing, Inc.
www.SirenPublishing.com